GRETA
AND THE
GHOST
HUNTERS

Other titles by
SAM COPELAND

Sam Copeland is an author, which has come as something of a shock to him. He is from Manchester and now lives in London with two smelly cats, three smelly children and one relatively clean-smelling wife. He is the author of the bestselling *Charlie Changes Into a Chicken* (which was shortlisted for the Waterstones Children's Book Prize), its two sequels, *Charlie Turns Into a T-Rex* and *Charlie Morphs Into a Mammoth*, and *Uma and the Answer to Absolutely Everything*. Despite legal threats, he refuses to stop writing.

Follow Sam online:
www.sam-copeland.com
@stubbleagent
#GretaGhostHunters

Sarah Horne has been an illustrator for over fifteen years. She started her career working for newspapers such as the *Guardian* and the *Independent on Sunday* and has since illustrated many funny young fiction titles. She works traditionally with a dip pen and Indian ink, and finishes the work digitally.

Follow Sarah online:
www.sarahhorne.studio
@sarahhorne9

GRETA
AND THE
GHOST
HUNTERS

SAM COPELAND

ILLUSTRATED BY Sarah Horne.

PUFFIN

PUFFIN BOOKS

UK | USA | Canada | Ireland | Australia
India | New Zealand | South Africa

Puffin Books is part of the Penguin Random House group of companies
whose addresses can be found at global.penguinrandomhouse.com.

www.penguin.co.uk
www.puffin.co.uk
www.ladybird.co.uk

First published 2022
001

Text copyright © Sam Copeland, 2022
Illustrations copyright © Sarah Horne, 2022

The moral right of the author and illustrator has been asserted

Text design by Ken De Silva
Printed and bound in Great Britain by Clays Ltd, Elcograf S.p.A.

A CIP catalogue record for this book is available from the British Library

The authorized representative in the EEA is Penguin Random House Ireland,
Morrison Chambers, 32 Nassau Street, Dublin DO2 YH68

ISBN: 978-0-241-44638-6

All correspondence to:
Puffin Books, Penguin Random House Children's
One Embassy Gardens, 8 Viaduct Gardens, London SW11 7BW

To the ghosts of my past –
my much missed grandparents
Sadie, Robert, Victor and Rachel,
and all the generations stretching
back through time.

Family Woebegone

PROLOGUE

Greta Woebegone did not believe in ghosts because she was a sensible young girl and sensible young girls tend not to believe in ghosts. That was until the day she was knocked over by a car and died, when everything changed.

But do not be too alarmed. Greta Woebegone did not die for long. You see, the thing about Greta is that she is surprisingly indestructible, and a Volkswagen Passat proved to be no match for her.

But we shall not be starting our story at the scene of an automobile accident. That would be far too dramatic, and this is not that type of book. This is a very serious novel full of *important themes* and *valuable moral lessons*, and not one of easy thrills and cheap laughs. Instead we shall begin by introducing the characters, and build up to the 'little car incident', as it became known in the Woebegone household.

So who belongs to this Woebegone household? Excellent question, assiduous reader.

You have already met Greta Woebegone. She is ten years old, small and unimportant-looking. Beyond that, I am not sure what to say about her – you children all look the same to me. She is, though, the main character of this book unfortunately. And why 'unfortunately'? Because Greta Woebegone is rather dull.

'No, I'm not!' Greta might argue, if it was her turn to talk, which it isn't. 'I'm actually rather interesting. I have brown hair. I love dogs and football. My favourite subject is –'

Stop interrupting, Greta. Wait your turn.

Greta lives in Woebegone Hall – a grand name for not such a grand house. The name was given to it by Greta's great-great-great-great-grandfather, a man high of aspiration and low of wealth. Woebegone Hall is a tall tombstone of a building, a great weathered slab of grey stone peppered with cobwebbed windows.

It has four bedrooms, and Greta's bedroom looks out over the small back garden, the graveyard beyond, where many of the Woebegone family are buried, and on to the factories in the distance.

Greta's brother (even more small and insignificant than his sister) has the bedroom next to hers. He is three years old. I cannot at this moment recall his name. If it were his turn to speak, he would probably say something about lorries or some such. I don't really know – I try not to listen to him.

Greta is fortunate enough to still have both her parents. Her father, William Woebegone, uses a wheelchair, smokes a pipe, has a large beard and moustache, and is always working on his latest collection of poetry. Her mother, Prosecca, also smokes a pipe but has neither beard nor moustache. She does have dyed purple hair, however, and loves yoga, crystals and chanting. And whenever Prosecca chants, William closes his eyes and furrows his brow as if in great pain.

That leaves Mildred Woebegone – or Grandma Woebegone, as she is more commonly known – both ancient family matriarch and Greta's best friend. Grandma Woebegone lives in the attic, because that is where old women live in stories, even though it is extremely impractical and dangerous to give them rooms at the top of so many rickety stairs. She has a world-record-sized marble collection, and many, many years ago was a racing driver – and a very good one too.

She was all set to race in the World Championship before an accident destroyed her car and left her with a broken arm, and her husband, George Woebegone, made her stop, which was something that husbands could do to their wives in those days.

Grandma Woebegone's bedroom is dotted with black-and-white photographs of her standing next to her racing car, shaking bottles of champagne, laurel wreaths round her neck, and several old trophies that gather dust on her shelf.

Grandma Woebegone is also convinced she can speak to ghosts. This is nonsense. The rest of the family all know there is nothing haunted about their house. The strange chills they all feel from time to time are just draughts. The weird clunks and creaks that rattle the house at night are just pipes. The creeping sense of dread that shivers up their necks whenever they go into the cellar is just rising damp. And the awful smells that occasionally fill the house are merely coming from the nappy of Greta's little brother (this is true – those nappies are undeniably dreadful).

Finally there is a cowardly ginger cat called Pussy Lanimous. When not hiding under a bed or in wardrobes, it wees on the rugs and fails to catch the mice that scuttle around the house whenever the lights go out, which they regularly do.

And that is everybody you need to know about right now. Well, not quite everybody . . . So who am I? Ah, *that* is the question. But one that will be answered later. For now I shall retreat into the background and allow this little story to unfold.

We begin on a biting grey morning deep in the cold heart of November, as Greta Woebegone makes her entrance . . .

CHAPTER
1

Greta Woebegone ran up the stairs of Woebegone Hall two at a time. It still took her quite a while to reach the top because there were a lot of them. She burst into the attic and there was Grandma Woebegone, sitting in the bed she rarely had the strength to leave, wearing a lacy nightie and round purple sunglasses (which 'helped her see the spirits').

'Quietly, dear! You startled Grandpa,' Grandma Woebegone whispered, pointing to an empty space next to the bed.

'Hi, Grandpa!' Greta waved to the empty space next to the bed. 'How are you today?'

Greta had no memory of her grandfather, who

had died not long after she was born.

Grandma Woebegone cocked her bespectacled head towards the empty space, listening hard.

'He says he's very well, thank you. He says he'd love to hear you play the recorder later.'

This ought to have been a giveaway that Grandma could not, in fact, talk to ghosts. No adult, living or dead, ever truly wants to listen to a child play the recorder.

'And,' Grandma Woebegone continued, a smile wrinkling her face as she pulled out a small parcel from under her pillow, 'he says "Happy Birthday!"'

'Thanks, Grandpa!' Greta beamed. 'And thank you, Grandma.' Greta took the present and gave her grandma a warm hug.

Grandma Woebegone grinned. 'Well, go on then! Open it!'

Greta tore at the wrapping paper and three presents fell into her lap.

They were: a half-used roll of Sellotape, a tin of kidney beans and a calendar entitled *The World's Most Spectacular Wheelbarrows*.

Greta did her best to push a grateful smile on to her face. 'Lovely!' she said. 'I mean, great! But . . . but . . . why did –'

Grandma gave her a knowing wink. 'Grandpa told me you like wheelbarrows at the moment.'

'Did he now? Thanks, Grandpa.' Greta gave two thumbs up to the empty space next to the bed.

'He says you're very welcome,' Grandma said, patting Greta's leg.

'And the Sellotape is . . . ?'

'To stick the pictures of the wheelbarrows up when the calendar is finished.'

'Of course,' said Greta, nodding. 'So thoughtful. And – yum – kidney beans too. You shouldn't have, Grandma. Really.'

'Your favourite.'

'My favourite.'

They were not Greta's favourite. In fact, anybody who says kidney beans are their favourites are enormous liars who probably secretly snaffle whole chocolate eggs when they think nobody is looking.

It was doubly unfortunate that not only were the kidney beans and Sellotape terrible presents, they were also the cause of Greta's death. The world's most spectacular wheelbarrows were not to blame.

'Thanks for all my presents, Grandma. They're brilliant,' white-lied Greta, giving her grandmother another hug. 'Bye for now! And bye, Grandpa!'

Greta waved again at the empty space and, clutching her presents, skipped out of the room and downstairs to the kitchen where her parents were both smoking their pipes. The kitchen was warm, and eggs and sausages were frying on the stove.

'So what did the old crackpot get you this time?'

Greta's father asked.

'Darling,' Greta's mother said, examining her nails. 'Don't call your mother that in front of Greta. You know how the child gets upset at the slightest thing. Anyway, it's your mother's chakras – they are totally misaligned.'

'Nonsense! Greta knows my mother's both old and a crackpot,' her husband replied. 'Isn't that right, Greta?'

Greta said nothing to this, and her father continued. 'Well, out with it. What did she get you?'

'A calendar of wheelbarrows, a tin of kidney beans and some Sellotape,' Greta said in a small voice, dumping the calendar and kidney beans on the kitchen table, and absent-mindedly pocketing the Sellotape.

'You see? I rest my case. Bonkers as a box of frogs. And was she talking to herself again?'

Greta gave a small nod. 'Yes. Lots,' she replied, looking at the floor.

Greta's mother shook her head. 'It's getting worse.'

'Yes. She's absolutely lost her marbles,' Greta's father said.

'And it was such a huge collection . . .' replied her mother. 'It's definitely time,' she added, giving her husband a look.

'Time for what?' Greta asked.

'Well,' her father said, 'to look into somewhere else for her to live. A home.'

Greta gasped. 'No! You can't! *This* is her home!'

'It might be for the best, darling,' her mother said. 'She isn't getting any younger. She needs help with her finances. All those old trophies could be sold. And she shouldn't own this great big house. It's too much for her to handle. It should be taken off her hands. And placed into ours. With the curtains open, her bedroom has a glorious view and would make a *divine* yoga studio . . .'

Before Greta had time to gasp again, her mother continued. 'Now do me a favour, darling – run to the shop and get some mince and tomatoes. I want to put those kidney beans to good use and make chilli con carne.'

And, just like that, Greta's fate was sealed.

It was not far to the shop. Out of the house,

down the hill, turn left, turn right and you're there. Greta zipped up her parka, put on her bobble hat and gloves, and slammed the door behind her.

It was cold and wet, the leaves slippy underfoot, and it was going to be a day that never felt quite like the sun had risen. Greta hopped on her bike and started down the hill. The wind rushed round her ears as she gathered speed.

Within sight of the house still, her mind full of thoughts of her grandmother being carted off to a nursing home, Greta didn't notice the Sellotape fall out of her pocket.

It bounced under her back wheel, knocking Greta immediately out of control. The bike wobbled perilously, then careered on to the other side of the road –

And straight into the path of a Volkswagen Passat.

She had no memory of what happened next. The driver had no time to stop; Greta's heart had stopped by the time she hit the ground.

It did not start again for very nearly two minutes, during which time Greta was very much dead.

The bike lay on its side, the back wheel spinning, and everything was silent but for the ticking of the car engine.

But then, as the crowds gathered round her, pointing and whispering, Greta's heart started beating again. She gasped in a great lungful of air, sat bolt upright, and gave a huge scream, which rather surprised and upset the onlookers. And then she collapsed back down, unconscious, in which state she remained for many days.

CHAPTER 2

Greta remembered almost nothing of her time in hospital – just a faint distant beeping and a disinfectant smell that she could not shift from her pyjamas afterwards.

After a few days, she was allowed home to recover. November turned into December, and the light that leaked into Greta's bedroom became dimmer. The only sounds that drifted in from outside were the clattering of her brother playing with his toy lorries and the mechanical whirring of her father going up and down the stairlift. Her parents dropped food into her room three times a day but were always too busy for anything more than the briefest of chats.

Greta became weary of looking at the same

view: her dresser, her wardrobe and her Whoopsie-Daisy – a terrifying doll with long arms, wide eyes and a 'natural toilet action', which said 'Whoopsie-daisy!' if it was dropped on the floor. She had read every one of her books and while part of her wondered if she might be strong enough now to make her usual trip to the library to replace them, another bigger part told her that it was probably more sensible to stay inside a bit longer.

Once, Greta's mother accidentally left a brochure in her room for somewhere called *St Atilla's Delightful Home for the Aged and Weak of Brain*. Reading that broke the tedium, until, with a flash of horror, Greta realized it was exactly this sort of place that her parents wanted to send Grandma. It was full of pictures of old people playing table tennis and painting, with fixed smiles on their faces. Greta could almost hear the staff barking orders at them to smile for the photograph.

Each morning and evening, her grandmother would rap on the floorboards of the room above and Greta would give two sharp blasts on her recorder in reply. She couldn't help wonder if that was the only conversation Grandma was getting these days.

Eventually Greta felt strong enough to get out of bed. Putting one foot on the cold floor, then the next, she pulled herself upright. She wobbled out of her room on newborn-calf legs, then turned back and opened her drawer and pulled out the one thing guaranteed to bring a smile to Grandma's face – her recorder.

Greta hobbled slowly upstairs, and gently knocked on her grandmother's door.

'Come in! Come in!'

Greta burst in and fell into the open arms of her grandmother.

'Oh, my darling! We missed you so much!' Grandma sobbed. 'Grandpa has been so worried.'

Greta smiled. 'And how is Grandpa?' she asked, shivering slightly at the cold.

'He's very well indeed,' Grandma Woebegone

replied. 'And,' she added, nodding at the recorder clutched in Greta's hand, 'he would dearly love to hear you play.'

'No, he bloomin' well would *not*!'

Greta nearly jumped out of her skin. The voice had come from behind her. A man's voice.

She swung round to see an old man standing beside the door. An old man who looked remarkably familiar.

Greta's mouth fell open.

'Your grandpa *loves* the recorder,' said Grandma, clapping her hands.

'No, I don't, you daft old bat!' the man said. 'It's an awful racket! Sounds like an angry cat stuck in a box with an even angrier chimpanzee!'

Greta's jaw dropped even nearer to the floor.

'G-G-Grandpa . . . ?'

'Yes, he's listening, dear,' said Grandma, smiling. 'Now go on! Play "*Greensleeves*" – he says he loves that one.'

'Oh, do be quiet, you silly woman!' the old man snapped. He pointed a long, bony finger at Greta.

'And you! Don't you DARE play that infernal recorder! If you know what's good for you, that is.'

'Is that r-r-really you?' stammered Greta.

'Of course it is, you dim-witted child! Do you not remember your own grandfather? Though I suppose you were rather small when I died.'

Greta sat down sharply on the bed. 'I must be going doolally. You're . . . *dead*. And I can see through you. Sort of. If I squint.'

'Yes, I'm dead! What's wrong with you? Are you always this dense or is it the result of the accident?'

'Who's dead, dear?' Grandma asked Greta.

Greta turned to her grandmother. 'I can . . . see him.'

'See who?'

'Grandpa!'

'You can see Grandpa?'

'Yes!'

'Actually see him?' Grandma eyed Greta suspiciously.

'Yes! And hear him.'

'Why . . . that makes two of us then . . .'

Grandma said uncertainly.

'Stuff and nonsense!' growled Grandpa. 'She never listened to a word I said when I was alive, and she certainly can't hear me now I'm dead! And as for seeing me . . .'

Grandpa Woebegone walked over to Grandma and started dancing in front of her. 'Look, you old fraud! You can't see me! You can't see me!' he shouted, hopping from one foot to the other.

'It's wonderful news, isn't it, Grandpa?' Grandma said, turning in completely the opposite direction. 'Our granddaughter has the sight! Just like me!'

'You see!' Grandpa said, throwing his hands into the air. 'She's totally and utterly clueless!'

'But . . . you're . . . you're a . . . ghost,' stammered Greta.

'Well done, child! Get top marks in Stating the Totally Obvious lessons at school, did you?'

'This doesn't make any sense. It must be some result of the accident! All in my mind. Maybe I just need to . . .'

Greta shook her head like a dog getting out

of a bath, her eyes clamped shut.

'Nope. I'm still here,' Grandpa Woebegone said, appearing right in front of her.

'Argh!' shouted Greta. 'But . . . but . . . ghosts don't exist!'

'Of course they do!' Grandma said, smiling. 'Your grandpa is standing right there,' she added, again pointing at completely the wrong part of the room.

Greta put her head in her hands. 'I don't feel well,' she groaned. 'I need a lie-down.'

She stood up, rubbing her eyes. 'I'll come and see you later when I'm feeling better, Grandma.'

'All right, dear. Go and get some rest.'

'And you,' Greta said, pointing at Grandpa Woebegone, 'do NOT exist.'

'Course I don't,' replied Grandpa Woebegone sarcastically. 'That's why you can't see me, hear me or talk to me.'

'Argh!' Greta arghed.

She ran out of the attic and down the stairs into her room, slammed the door and flumped on to her bed. She pulled the duvet over her against the chill and lay there panting, trying to get her head around what she had just seen.

It couldn't be real, could it? Had she actually just seen a *ghost*?

She closed her eyes and breathed deeply. The longer she lay there, the more she realized she must have imagined the whole thing.

There were no such things as ghosts.

Absolutely not.

Feeling calmer now, Greta opened her eyes.

'Hello there,' said the small pale boy standing beside her.

'ARGH!!!' Greta arghed *again*, nearly falling out of bed in shock. 'WHO ON EARTH ARE YOU?'

'I'm Percy. Percy Woebegone.'

'WELL, WHY ARE YOU IN MY ROOM?'

'I think you'll find it was my room before it was yours.'

'What are you talking about?' asked Greta. 'When was this your room?'

Percy frowned thoughtfully. 'I had it from 1583 until 1591. When I died.'

CHAPTER 3

'You're a ghost!' Greta groaned.

'I prefer the term "no-body".'

'Ha! That's it! I've completely lost my mind! I'm seeing dead people everywhere!'

'Prithee!' Percy covered his ears. 'Do not use the D-word. It is so . . . final.'

'WHY IS THIS HAPPENING TO ME?' Greta shouted at the ceiling. 'WHY AM I SEEING GHOSTS?'

'NOT *GHOSTS*! NO-BODIES!' shouted Percy.

'GET OUT OF MY HEAD!' shouted Greta.

'I'M NOT IN YOUR HEAD!'

'YOU'RE NOT REAL!'

'I *AM* REAL! AND WHY ARE WE SHOUTING?'

Greta slumped back on her bed, breathing hard.

'OK,' she said after a while. 'Let's just say you *are* real. Then maybe Grandpa is real. That means I can see ghosts. That means ghosts are real.'

And at that thought it all became a little much for poor Greta, and she started crying.

A look of concern crossed Percy's face. 'Ah, now, don't weep! 'Tis not all bad.'

'It *is* all bad! I can see ghosts! Mother and Father'll want to lock me up too, like they want to do to poor Grandma!'

'Come, come!' said Percy. 'It could be worse! In my day they would have burned you as a witch.' Percy suddenly glared at Greta. 'You're not a witch, are you?'

Greta sniffed. 'No, I'm not!'

'But you *can* see me.'

'I am *not* a witch!'

'Hmm,' said Percy. 'I shall give you the benefit of the doubt. For now.'

'Thank you so much,' said Greta without really meaning it.

'My pleasure. Now then, why don't we play a

cheering game to lift our spirits?'

'I think I've had quite enough spirits for one day,' Greta said.

Percy looked at her blankly.

'Fine,' Greta said, wiping her eyes. 'What type of game?'

'Well . . . How's about a game of Stick-Push-a-Poo?'

'What's that?'

'It's where we each have a stick and we find a poo, and then we push the poo with our sticks.'

'That doesn't sound *that* much fun really,' said Greta, trying to be polite but struggling.

'Well then . . .' said Percy, scratching his head. 'Mayhap we could play a few rounds of good old Sticky-Stick-Stick?'

'What's Sticky-Stick-Stick?'

'It is where we each have a stick and we find another stick, and then we push the stick with our sticks.'

'That actually sounds worse than Stick-Push-a-Poo! Does *everything* you play involve sticks?'

'No! We could play . . . We could play . . . I know! Why don't we play Thrash-a-Boy? You'll *love* that!'

'Great! How do we play it?' asked Greta.

'We go outside, then we find a really poor peasant child and we thrash them. With a stick.'

'WHAT?! No! That sounds dreadful! And cruel. And it still involves sticks. You are absolutely stick-obsessed.'

'I am not! Forsooth, let us then play a game of Eggs-Box!'

Greta's eyes widened. 'You have an Xbox?'

'Ah. No. Dash it, I have neither eggs nor box! Thwarted at the first step.'

Greta let out a loud groan again.

'And anyway,' continued Percy, 'I fear I may not be able to play any of those games with you.'

'Why not?'

'Because it is difficult for me to touch anything in your world. You know, being a no-body.'

'WELL, WHY DID YOU SUGGEST PLAYING THEM THEN?' roared Greta.

'There is no need to shout –'

'Hang on a moment,' said Greta, holding up a finger. 'If you can't touch anything, how come you don't just fall through the floor? And keep falling? Until you hit Australia?'

This was an excellent question, and one to which even I have no answer.

'What is an *Australia*?' asked Percy.

This was not an excellent question. But it was a perfectly reasonable one from somebody who died almost two hundred years before Captain Cook landed on the shores of Australia.

Greta ignored the question and returned with one of her own.

'Did you say your name was Percy Woebegone?'

Percy nodded.

'Does that mean you're my relation?' Greta asked, eyes wide.

'Yes, I suppose it must do. A distant one at least.'

Greta was rather pleased he was a distant relation – he didn't seem the brightest. And now she looked closer at his pale face, she could see it was marked with several unpleasant-looking boils.

She suddenly gave an involuntary shiver.

'Why is it *so* cold?'

'Ah, yes. Terribly sorry,' apologized Percy. ''Tis my fault. Whenever I enter a room, the temperature drops.'

'Well, can you stop it?'

'There is nothing I can do. I cannot control it!'

'Well, it's not very nice!'

'Verily, but 'tis worse for me. Every time I enter a room, people start shivering,' Percy said, looking down. 'Oh, woe!'

Greta was beginning to feel sorry for Percy.

'And because I cannot pick things up,' Percy continued, 'I have not been able to hit any poor people with sticks for many a year! Oh, woe is me!'

'YOU KNOW YOU REALLY ARE QUITE HORRID AND –'

'What's all this shouting about?'

Greta's mother had opened the door of the bedroom and was peering in.

'Er . . . nothing,' Greta replied, eyes darting towards Percy, who seemed to be holding his breath.

'Are you talking to yourself?' Greta's mother said with a glare. 'Because it's awful enough having her upstairs talking to herself all the time. She's a bad influence on you. We need her out of here as fast as possible. And this room is freezing! It's your negative chakras, Greta, dear. You really *must* do something to improve them.'

And with that she flounced out of the room.

'I am pretty certain that crone be a witch,' said Percy, nodding at Greta's mother.

'She's *not* a crone!' whispered Greta, doubting herself even as she said it. 'Or a witch!'

'Who's not a witch, darling?' said Greta's mother, poking her head back round the door.

'Nobody!' said Greta, and she gave what she hoped was an innocent smile.

'Hmm,' said Greta's mother, narrowing her eyes, and she flounced off again (but properly this time).

I am afraid to say that Greta created quite the scene then. It was all snivels and sniffs and, 'Poor Grandma, poor me, I'm losing my best friend, boohoohoo'.

Now, quite why a ten-year-old child would be best friends with an old lady who smelled faintly of freshly dug-up radishes, I do not know.

'Perchance I might be of help?' Percy asked, looking at Greta with unnecessary sympathy.

Greta looked up, eyes full of tears, and whispered, 'I don't think so. You see, they are going to take Grandma away. Lock her up in a home.'

'That is terrible!' said Percy, gasping. 'But I have a plan to prevent it . . .'

Greta sat up. 'Really? What?'

'This is what you do: on the coldest day of winter, you take your grandmother up to the top of the highest hill in the vicinity.'

'Yes . . . ? Then what?'

'And then you leave her there.'

'You want me to leave Grandma on top of a mountain on the coldest day of the year?'

'That is correct. And make sure not to take any food or water.'

Greta gasped. 'But . . . but . . . that would kill her!'

'That's right. It really is the best way to deal with a witch.'

'How dare you! Grandma is NOT a witch! And she's *your* relative as well!'

'Yes, I know! And having a witch in the family brings great shame upon our name,' said Percy, shaking his head.

'Not *everybody* is a witch, you know.'

'Oh, come, come! Look at her! Of course she is a witch. She has hairy moles and talks to ghosts!'

'*I'M* TALKING TO A GHOST!'

'Yes, but you do not have hairy moles.' Percy suddenly glared at Greta suspiciously – the second such glare Greta had received in the same number of minutes. 'Unless you are hiding them?'

Percy started trying to peer down Greta's collar.

'Let me see if you are concealing –'

Greta stepped away. 'Stop that! Right, I'd really like you to leave my room now! I need to think of a way to stop them sending Grandma away.'

'Fine, forsooth! Well, come not to me looking for any more help!' shouted Percy.

'Oh, don't worry, I WON'T!' shout-whispered Greta.

And she was true to her word.

Although not for long. Because the very next day she came up with an idea to save her grandmother for which she really needed the help of the witch-obsessed numbskull, Percy Woebegone . . .

CHAPTER
4

'I am full weary of you calling me a numbskull!' shouted Percy.

'But you *are* a numbskull,' said Grandpa. 'It's simply a fact.'

'CAN YOU TWO STOP ARGUING FOR JUST ONE MINUTE!' roared Greta.

She had only gathered the two ghosts in the kitchen to tell them her plan five minutes ago, but already she was regretting it. Not least because two ghosts made it doubly cold and she had had to put on her bobble hat to stop her ears freezing – but, worse, it was immediately clear that the ghosts did not get on. At all.

The plan had occurred to her just after breakfast.

Her brother had finished his food and been sent to his room. Greta's father was wheeling around the kitchen, looking for his pipe.

'You've tidied it away again, haven't you?' he said with a sigh, looking at Greta's mother.

'I haven't touched it! You've just forgotten where you've put it. You're as bad as your mother. Speaking of which,' she said, adjusting her crystal necklace, 'I heard the old goat talking to herself again last night. Enough is enough.'

Greta's heart gave a lurch and she dropped her spoon into her bowl with a clatter.

'She's not,' she said quietly.

Greta's parents turned to her, and Greta swallowed.

'Not what, darling?'

'She's not talking to herself,' Greta said. 'She's talking to Grandpa.'

Greta's parents stared at her for a moment. And then both burst out laughing.

'Oh, darling,' Greta's mother said. 'You *are* funny!' She wiped a non-existent tear of laughter away from the corner of her eye.

'I'm not being funny! Grandma *isn't* losing her mind! It's this house. It's haunted. She's talking to *actual* ghosts and I can see them too! Ever since I had my accident!' Greta said.

'Absolute hogwash! There's no such thing as ghosts,' said her father. 'The problem is you've spent too long locked up inside these walls.'

Greta's stomach lurched at the thought of going outside.

'And I don't want Grandma encouraging you any more with this ghost nonsense. This is *her* fault,' Greta's mother snapped, grabbing her car keys.

'But –'

'Enough!' her mother said, holding her hand up. 'This discussion has finished! It is a nonversation. Now, come on, darling,' she said, turning to her husband. 'We're due to view St Atilla's at eleven.

Perhaps they can take her this week – before she does any more damage.' She looked at Greta. 'And we should probably take you to the doctor's too. Get you checked out.'

Just then the doorbell rang. Her mother answered it and, a moment later, she returned.

'It's that child from down the road. Emily.'

Greta's eyes lit up.

'She wants to know if you'd like to play out,' her mother continued.

The light in Greta's eyes dimmed and she looked at the window nervously.

'No,' she said quickly. 'I . . . I don't think I'm quite strong enough for that yet.'

'But you haven't been outside since the accident,' her father said. 'Not even to the library. Fresh air might do you good.'

'I told you, I can't go out!' Greta blurted and rushed out of the room.

Ten minutes later, her parents were driving off in the car and Greta was sitting on her grandma's bed, looking extremely forlorn.

'Don't worry, my dear,' Grandma Woebegone said, patting her arm. 'It'll be all right.'

'It won't! They are absolutely set on putting you in a home!'

'Well, maybe it's for the best. I don't want to be a trouble to anyone.'

'You're not trouble! You're part of this family. And I don't want you to go.'

They both sat in silence.

'They say you talk to yourself,' continued Greta. 'And that you're a bad influence on me.'

'But you know I'm not talking to myself. I'm talking to Grandpa.'

'No, she's not!' Grandpa Woebegone suddenly said, causing Greta to jump so high she nearly fell off the bed.

'How long have *you* been here?' Greta asked Grandpa.

'Oooh, many years,' Grandma replied. 'I first moved in – now, let me think . . .'

'NOT YOU, MILDRED, YOU WRINKLY OLD WOMBAT! SHE'S ASKING ME!' Grandpa shouted.

'My, my,' continued Grandma. 'It must be close to forty years ago now . . .'

'You see!' Grandpa said, shaking his head. 'She's no idea I'm here, the old fraud!'

'No, Grandma. I'm talking to Grandpa!'

Grandma smiled at Greta. 'Of course you are, dear.'

'She doesn't believe you can see me,' Grandpa said. 'Tell her that you know all about her secret snail farm under the bed!'

'*What* did you say?' asked Greta. 'A secret *snail farm*?'

Grandma gasped. 'How do you know about that?'

'Grandpa just told me!'

'So you really *can* see him?' asked Grandma, eyes wide in shock.

'Yes! He's stood right there,' Greta said, pointing.

'I told you she didn't believe you,' Grandpa said. 'Because *she* can't see me. You're the only one who *actually* can.'

And that's when the idea of how she might save her grandma finally clawed its way out of Greta's brain.

She gasped and stood bolt upright. 'Meet me in the kitchen in five minutes,' she said.

'But I can't get all the way downstairs, love,' Grandma said.

'NOT YOU, YOU CRUSTY OLD CRAB!' shouted Grandpa Woebegone. 'SHE'S TALKING TO ME!'

Seven minutes later, Greta was sitting at the kitchen table, head in her hands. She couldn't believe she needed help from two ghosts who were, well, the absolute *worst.*

'Please stop arguing,' she groaned.

'Well, he started it!' Grandpa Woebegone said.

'I did not! You called me a numbskull.'

'Well, you are! Look!' Grandpa lifted his foot, pointing to the sole of his ghost shoe. 'You keep leaving dog doings all over the place from your games of Stick-Push-a-Poo!'

'I do not!'

'JUST STOP IT, YOU TWO!' shouted Greta, pulling at her hair. 'If you weren't already dead, I would strangle the pair of you!'

Silence fell across the kitchen. Grandpa and Percy stared open-mouthed at Greta.

'Thank you. *Finally.* Now. I need some help from the both of you.'

'And, prithee, why should we help you after you have just shouted at us as if we were no more than a pair of pigeon-livered, knotty-pated fools?' Percy asked.

'A pair of *what?*' asked Greta.

'He does that sometimes,' Grandpa said. 'Gets overexcited with his Shakespearean insults. Best to just ignore him.'

Greta took the advice and continued. 'My mother and father are going to stick Grandma in an old people's home because they think she has lost her marbles and is talking to herself.'

'Good riddance!' said Grandpa, nodding firmly.

You might say to yourself at this point, 'No! Surely nobody can be that horrible! He can't have *actually* meant "good riddance" to his wife?!'

It is my grim duty to inform you that he absolutely did. For now at least.

Greta, however, chose to ignore the comment – or perhaps she was not able to believe that such meanness existed, so blanked it out.

'So here's what I need you to do,' she said. 'I need you to prove to my parents that you exist – that *ghosts* exist – so they'll know Grandma isn't talking to herself. Then she won't have to leave.'

'But she can't see ghosts,' Grandpa said. 'So, technically, she does talk to herself. Why don't you just tell them she's lying and can't actually see us?'

Greta thought about the gleam in her mother's eye when she had talked about turning Grandma's bedroom into a yoga studio.

'Somehow I don't think that will be enough,' said Greta. 'But if I can prove that this house actually has two ghosts in it –'

'Three,' corrected Grandpa.

'Pardon?' asked Greta, blinking.

'Three. There are three ghosts in this house.'

CHAPTER
5

'What,' Greta asked, 'did you just say?'

Grandpa Woebegone scowled. 'Are you deaf? I said there's three ghosts in the house. Us two and the one in the cellar. Have you not met him yet?'

Greta shook her head.

Percy gasped. 'Well, don't! You mustn't go down there! That no-body is very, *very* bad.'

'He's right,' said Grandpa, a shadow crossing his face. 'That one can be a bit –'

'Oh, woe, woe and thrice woe!' wailed Percy. 'For that no-body is a lump of foul deformity, unfit for any place but hell!'

'Yes,' said Grandfather. 'We get the picture. You see? Always overexcited with his insults. Anyway, let's just say you should definitely avoid that ghost if you can.'

'I really have no intention of meeting any more ghosts, thank you. Two is quite enough,' said Greta primly.

Well, prim Miss Greta Woebegone, you might not *intend* to meet any more ghosts, but you are going to.

Just not yet.

'So, let's focus on the plan. Can you make my parents see you so that they'll believe Grandma can talk to ghosts and not send her off to a care home?'

Percy was the first to answer. 'Perchance. We can try. But only if you prove to me first that your grandmother is not a witch. I cannot help her if she be a witch.'

'I've told you she's not a witch!'

'So you say. But if you want my help, you must prove it.'

'But . . . but . . . how on earth do I prove that Grandma's not a witch?'

'Well,' said Percy matter-of-factly. 'The simplest way is to go to a local pond or lake, and throw her in.'

'I am *not* throwing my grandma in a lake, thank you very much!' said Greta, getting increasingly exasperated. 'And anyway, why would that tell you if she's a witch?'

'If she floats, she is a witch; if she sinks and drowns, she is not. 'Tis the only certain way to tell.'

'That's ridiculous. Grandpa, you were married to her, you know she isn't a witch! Tell him.'

Grandpa Woebegone sucked his teeth. 'You can never be a hundred per cent certain about these things.'

'Grandpa!' scolded Greta. 'Tell him! NOW!'

'Fine! She isn't a witch. Happy?' harrumphed Grandpa.

'Thank you,' nodded Greta. 'Good enough for

you, Percy? Will you help?'

Percy thought for a long moment, then gave a deep bow. 'I shall do my best to help you, my new friend and kinswoman, and your grandmother. Who is still possibly a witch.'

'Excellent. And you, Grandpa? Will you help?'

Grandpa Woebegone gave Greta a gentle smile. 'Dearest, sweet grandchild. Of *course* I'm not going to help.'

'WHAT? WHAT DO YOU MEAN? SHE'S YOUR WIFE! YOU SPENT YOUR WHOLE LIFE TOGETHER!'

'Exactly. It's my chance to finally get rid of her!'

'Grandpa Woebegone! You are the meanest, most miserable grandparent in the whole world!'

Grandpa grinned happily.

Greta decided to try a new tack. 'You do realize,

Grandpa, that if Grandma dies an unhappy death, she might come back as a ghost too and haunt this house. Which means you'd be stuck with her *forever*.'

Grandpa closed his eyes and considered.

'It's too dangerous. If we haunt your parents, it will bring trouble! Mark my words. It's best just to lead a quiet life. Keep your head down, I always say.'

'Grandpa. You'll be stuck with her,' Greta repeated slowly, 'forever.'

'Gah! Fine. You win. We'll regret it, though, you'll see!'

'Splendid!' said Percy. 'So now we just need to work out how to start haunting the life out of your mother and father!'

Greta gasped. 'I don't want you to kill them! Just scare them a bit!'

Percy looked at Greta as if she had lost her mind. 'It was just a *phrase*. Obviously we're not going to *kill* them.'

More's the pity.

It did not take long for Greta and Percy to formulate

a plan.

And was the plan formulated by Greta and Percy a good one?

Of course not.

'I know what we can do,' said Percy. 'Watch this!'

He closed his eyes and began to concentrate.

Greta felt a tiny draught blow across her neck and the light bulb above her head flickered.

'There!' said Percy, grinning.

'Is that it?' Greta asked.

'What do you mean "Is that it?"? Didst thou not find it spooky?'

'Yes, I did,' Greta lied. 'It was quite spooky.'

'*Quite* spooky?' Percy asked, narrowing his eyes.

'Very spooky, I mean!'

'You do not look greatly spooked.'

'No, honestly, I am,' Greta white-lied again, giving a fake shiver for good measure.

It was a display only an idiot would fall for.

'Excellent!' said Percy, falling for the display. 'For a moment I thought you did not find it spooky.'

'Oh no, not at all! Flickering light bulb. Classic

haunted house stuff. That's *so* high up on the spooky chart.'

Percy beamed.

'Ha!' Grandpa laughed. 'That was about as scary as Mildred's bloomers!'

Greta wasn't sure whether her grandma's bloomers were scary or not – or, indeed, what exactly bloomers even were.

'Don't listen to him, Percy. It was very good,' she said gently. 'I just wonder if you could make it a little more . . . dramatic?'

'You wish me to make the lights more a-flickery?' Percy asked.

'Let's see how it looks.'

Percy closed his eyes again, concentrating hard. This time all the lights in the kitchen started flickering and flashing, the microwave pinged and whirred into life, and the radio started blaring, turning off and on.

'Now *that*,' said Greta, clapping her hands, 'is more like it. That should definitely do the trick. Now we just need to pick our moment . . . '

CHAPTER
6

And the moment Greta picked was the next day. Every month the mobile hairdresser came to Woebegone Hall, wheeling in a great hairdryer that looked like a space helmet, beneath which Greta's mother, Prosecca Woebegone, would sit doing leg stretches while watching yoga videos on her phone.

'So, while she's doing that, you come in and make the room cold, the lights flicker, and the hairdryer and phone turn off and on,' Greta said to Percy. 'That should be quite spooky enough to make her realize the house is haunted. You think you can manage it?'

Percy nodded solemnly in reply.

'He can't,' said Grandpa Woebegone. 'He'll mess it up.'

'Grandpa! Don't be so negative!' said Greta.

'You just wait and see. He'll make an absolute dog's dinner of it.'

Now, you might be asking at this point, 'Why is Grandpa Woebegone so mean and miserable?'

Let me just say this – you try being a ghost for years and years and years, seeing everything in your life wither and die, like a slow sad film you cannot stop watching, no matter how much you want to. Or, worse, going over all your mistakes and regrets again and again, not able to change them. It's enough to make anybody gloomy.

And what of Percy, then, you ask? Why is he so jolly?

Because he is an idiot, that's why.

Which is why he will indeed make a dog's dinner of it.

'He will not make a dog's dinner of it,' said Greta wrongly. 'I believe in him.' She smiled at Percy.

'Thank you. You know,' said Percy, smiling back

at Greta, 'I am starting to believe you might not be a witch after all.'

'Oh, pass me the sick bucket,' said Grandpa perfectly reasonably, 'and let's get on with this.'

They crept to the sitting room, where Greta's mother was chatting to the hairdresser. Her voice floated through the door, which was cracked open.

'Oh, yes, the minute she's out, I'll paint all the walls eggshell white, get the yoga mats down and start advertising classes. I'm even thinking of running gong bath sessions up there.'

'Egads, what's a gong bath session?' whispered Percy.

Greta shrugged and whispered, 'Dunno. Something yogic probably.'

'What's a yogic?' whispered Percy.

'Why are you whispering?' Grandpa asked Percy, speaking extra loudly to prove his point. 'They can't hear you.'

Greta pressed her eye to the crack in the door. She could see her mother on the phone, her purple hair under the huge, domed hairdryer.

'What on earth are you doing?' came a sudden voice from behind Greta, causing her to actually jump in the air.

It was her father.

'Erm, nothing!'

'It looked like you were peeking in that room,' he said, pointing with his pipe. 'Were you *spying* on your mother?'

'No! I was . . . I was . . .'

'Resting your face!' whispered Percy.

'I was resting my face!' Greta blurted out.

'You were resting your face . . . against a *door*?' her father asked, his voice full of suspicion.

Greta nodded and flashed a nervous smile.

'Hmm,' said her father. 'You're getting stranger by the day! Why don't you go outside and play?'

'I told you, I still feel too weak,' answered Greta quickly. Grandpa and Percy gave each other a knowing look.

'Fine,' said her father. 'Well, stop . . . resting your face against doors and go and do something more productive.' He wheeled off, muttering to himself.

'Phew!' said Percy. 'That was a close one. Lucky I was here to save the day.'

'"Resting your face",' said Grandpa, shaking his head in disbelief. 'Unbelievable . . .'

For once Greta found herself agreeing with her grandfather.

As soon as she heard the stairlift, which meant that her father was slowly winding his way up the stairs, Greta nodded to Percy. 'OK! It's time to spook my mother!'

Percy closed his eyes, his brow furrowing with concentration and his boils bulging alarmingly. Greta felt the hairs on the back of her neck prickle as the light above her flickered slightly.

'More,' she urged him.

Percy scrunched his face and strained. 'I'm trying!' he said.

'Trying for the loo by the looks of things,' said Grandpa.

Greta shushed her grandfather and turned back to peep through the gap in the door again.

And that's when it happened.

Percy scrunched his face even tighter, strained even more, and suddenly the lights started flashing. In the sitting room the lights were also flashing, as was Greta's mother's phone, which was turning on and off. And then, to Greta's great alarm, smoke began billowing out of the hairdryer hood.

With a scream, Greta's mother jumped out from under it, but it was too late – her hair was standing completely on end, frazzled and sizzling, as if she had just stuck her fingers in a plug socket.

Then, with an alarming *pop*, the hairdryer caught fire.

The screams of the hairdresser and Greta's mother were deafening as they tried to smother the flames with towels, but there was another noise beneath it that Greta couldn't quite put her finger on. A sort of distant whizzing noise.

A noise that seemed to be getting closer.

Quickly getting closer.

And then, with horror, it dawned on Greta what it was.

The stairlift!

She jumped up and ran down the hall to see the stairlift hurtling down the stairs at a terrifying speed at which no stairlift should ever be travelling.

Her father was clinging on to the arms for dear life, knuckles white, screaming through gritted teeth. 'NEEEEEEEEEEEEEEEEEEEAGGGGHHHHHH!'

The stairlift smashed into the bottom of the stairs, and Greta's father had just enough time to give Greta a look of utter terror before it shot off back up again, like a rocket strapped to the back of a missile.

'NOOOOOOOOOOO!' Greta's father screamed as the stairlift careered round the dog-leg bend in the stairs like a racing car.

'AIIIIEEEEEE!' Greta's mother screamed from the sitting room as smoke poured down the hall.

'Percy! Stop the haunting!' Greta yelled.

'I can't!' Percy wailed.

'Just try to calm yourself!'

'How?!'

The whizzing got louder as the out-of-control stairlift crashed to the bottom of the stairs once more then took off up again, Greta's father still screaming in terror.

'HELPPPPPP MEEEEEEEEEE!'

Grandpa roared with laughter. 'Oh, this is wonderful!'

And then, just as abruptly as it had started, it ended.

The lights stopped flickering, and the whizz of the stairlift reduced to the usual hum. The smell of smoke hung heavy in the air.

Slowly the stairlift crawled to the bottom of the stairs. Greta's father stared at Greta, open-mouthed. He then clambered away, into the wheelchair, and wheeled off, trembling and muttering to himself.

Grandpa, wheezing now, hooted, 'That's the funniest thing I've seen in years! He nearly killed both of them!'

'I did not!' Percy protested.

Greta turned to her grandpa and glared at him. 'It's not funny! Percy nearly did haunt the life out of them.'

'They're still alive, aren't they?' Grandpa said. 'I don't know what you're complaining about.'

'I suppose . . . Well, as long as the plan has worked, it will have been worth it,' Greta said.

'Of course it will have worked!' Percy said confidently.

Do *you* think it worked?

Exactly.

CHAPTER 7

Later that morning, Greta found her parents sitting together in silence in the appropriately named sitting room.

Greta sat down on the sofa opposite them. 'Are you both OK?' she asked gently.

'Do we *look* OK, darling?' her mother snapped, giving her daughter a look of simmering fury.

Greta did not have to answer. They did not look OK. Not in the slightest.

Her father was staring blankly into the distance, sipping from the glass of whisky in his still trembling hand. Her mother's purplish hair looked like she had parachuted out of a plane without a helmet, landed in a hedge and then been dragged through it backwards by a malfunctioning robot with blowtorches for fingers.

Silence once again cloaked the room. Eventually Greta plucked up the courage to speak.

'Maybe now you'll believe me and Grandma?'

'Believe what exactly?' her mother asked, peering at Greta through narrowed eyes.

'That –' Greta swallowed nervously – 'that this house is haunted.'

'*What?*' asked her mother, eyes widening in disbelief.

'It was ghosts that made all the electrics go wonky and that's why your hairdryer caught fire and the stairlift went –'

'What *on earth* are you babbling about?' interrupted her father. 'Ghosts? *Ghosts?* I've told you before that's all nonsense. Takes the biscuit.'

'But, Father, it was ghosts –'

'It was NOT ghosts. It was a faulty fuse. This house is so old the electrics are shot. The sooner we get hold of your grandmother's money to fix it, the better.'

'It wasn't a fuse, Father, it was –'

'That's enough!' her father roared. 'I want no more talk about ghosts in this house!'

'It's her upstairs,' Greta's mother said, pointing at the ceiling. 'She's a bad influence on Greta. Filling her head with ridiculous ideas.'

'Quite,' muttered her father.

'We have to get her out and into a care home before it gets any worse.'

'Quite,' repeated her father.

Greta stood up and walked quietly out.

She managed to hold her tears in until she got to her room, and then she buried the sound of her sobbing in her pillow.

Her plan had only made things worse.

A while later, Greta was sitting on her bedroom floor, her back pressed against the wall, eyes closed. The Whoopsie-Daisy doll stared down at her from the top of the wardrobe. Greta felt a shiver down her neck and opened her eyes to see Percy and Grandpa standing in front of her.

She groaned and closed her eyes again.

'Maybe when I open my eyes, you'll be gone. Maybe I'm losing my mind, like my mother thinks, and you aren't real. I just need to stop believing.'

She opened her eyes. Percy and Grandpa Woebegone were both still standing there.

'We're real, I'm afraid,' said Grandpa Woebegone.

Greta let out another groan.

'I am truly sorry about earlier, Greta,' said Percy. 'I tried my best.'

'You did, Percy. They just didn't believe it,' said Greta glumly. 'And I don't blame them – I hardly believe it myself. So please don't apologize. It's not your fault.'

'Yes, don't apologize, Percy,' said Grandpa. 'I haven't laughed as much as that since I died. Nearly split my sides! We should do it again. Soon. Anyway, must dash. Don't want your gloominess to spoil my jolly mood!' And out Grandpa went, walking through the closed bedroom door.

'He is such a mean-minded old grumblebum,' said Percy, shaking his head sadly. 'If he wasn't a man, I would *definitely* think he was a witch.'

Greta walked over to the window and stared out in silence. She longed to go outside, go to the shop and get a bag of pick 'n' mix, but the thought of it set her heart racing.

'You're right about Grandpa,' she said glumly.

'He's a witch? I knew it!'

She sighed. 'No! He's not a witch. But he is a mean-minded old grumblebum.'

'Yes. I think perhaps he died like that, and now he's stuck.'

'Percy, can I ask you a question?'

'Of course,' he replied. 'As long as it is not to gather frogspawn and a vial of children's tears for spells.'

'You do know that witches don't really exist?'

'Ah, that's exactly what *they* want you to believe,' Percy said, giving her a knowledgeable nod.

Greta didn't have an answer to this.

'Last week you did not believe that ghosts really exist,' added Percy. 'And yet here I am, stood in front of you.'

Again Greta found she had no answer.

'Anyway,' she said, 'I don't want you to gather frogspawn. I wanted to ask . . . if you don't mind, that is . . . do you know how you . . . died?'

'Of course I do!' replied Percy. ''Twas the plague.'

'Oh,' replied Greta. 'Was it . . . horrible?'

'Ah, 'twas not too bad.'

Greta blinked. 'Dying of the plague wasn't too bad?'

'Not really. Bit of sneezing and coughing, then, bang! Here I am. A no-body.' Percy gave a short laugh, then his face darkened. 'It was much worse watching the others get it.'

'Others?' Greta asked gently.

'Yes.' Percy turned to Greta, and she could see his eyes glistening with tears. 'It got my little sister first. That was tough. And then it got my mother. And then me. My father was never the same after that. That was the worst part of being a no-body. Watching him.'

'Oh, Percy. That's . . . terrible.'

Suddenly Greta's troubles seemed small in comparison.

And that's the thing – no matter how bad your problems are, you should always remember that life's supply of misery is endless and they could always get worse.

So next time you open your mouth to whine about your baby brother washing your favourite teddy bear in the toilet, close it again and get on with life. Because it's over far, far too soon.

'But that was just how life was in my day,' said

Percy. 'You just had to get on with it.'

'How do you mean?' asked Greta.

'Well, you had your little accident and –'

Greta bristled. 'I'd hardly call being knocked over by a car a "little accident".'

'When I was no more than four years of age, my uncle was run over by a horse and cart. And *he* just picked himself up, brushed himself down and carried on.' Percy nodded wisely. 'Sadly for him, he was still dizzy and walked straight in front of the next horse and cart that came along, and that killed him stone dead.'

'Oh,' said Greta, not sure what to add.

'And my Aunt Alice – she was relieving herself out of the upstairs window and fell out backwards. Died instantly.'

Greta gasped. 'That's terrible!'

'Even more terrible for Aunt Agnes, who was standing directly below the window at the time. She also died instantly.'

Greta gasped again.

'That was just what life was like then. Full of

danger. But you cannot hide away, Greta. Or else you miss what's worth living for.'

Greta turned back to the window and looked out on to the garden, and the graveyard beyond. She could faintly hear the sound of children playing in the distance. She closed her eyes, as if it pained her. I could feel her heart aching to go outside, but, underneath that, bubbling away, a cauldron of panic.

She opened her eyes again and looked at Percy. 'Percy, do you know why you're a ghost?'

'A no-body,' corrected Percy.

'Do you know why you're a no-body and your sister and mother aren't?'

Percy shook his head. 'I've been wondering that for hundreds of years.'

And Greta, being an insufferable goody two shoes who thought life was like a jolly Enid Blyton story, jumped up, clapped her hands and said, 'Well, *that's* a mystery we need to solve!'

CHAPTER
8

N ow, at this point you might have forgotten all about Greta's brother. Don't worry. Most people – including his family – forget him for days at a time. However, he is about to become important to the story. Which is unfortunate because I *still* cannot remember his name.

Embarrassing, I know. I shall for now have to call him Whats-his-name Woebegone. Or Whats for short.

Whats is rather like the mice that successfully avoid being caught by Pussy Lanimous. He is small, short-haired and says

very little, but squeaks occasionally while he happily scampers around Woebegone Hall.

And why will such an insignificant child become important to the story? We shall find out very shortly. But first, I am sorry to say, we must have another scene or two with Greta.

She awoke the next day still feeling very gloomy at the failure to spook her parents. Things were not made any better when Prosecca flung open Greta's curtains and told her to get out of bed, stop moping and go to the shops to buy pancakes and waffles for breakfast.

Despite her mood, there was nothing Greta enjoyed more than pancakes and waffles for breakfast, and she couldn't resist the temptation.

She had pulled her clothes on and wrapped up warm, but the moment she opened the front door she felt dizzy. Her legs turned to jelly at the sight of the main road. A car whizzed past and Greta thought she might faint.

Slowly she shut the door and trudged back

upstairs, dejected and defeated, and flumped on to Grandma Woebegone's bed.

'Oh, Grandma. Everything's wrong. And I'm afraid I've let you down,' she said accurately. 'I tried to prove to Mother and Father that ghosts exist. But it all went wrong when I asked a ghost called Percy to help, and it ended up nearly killing them both,' she continued, again accurately. 'And they *still* don't believe in ghosts.'

'Never mind, my dear. I'm sure you tried your best,' Grandma said. 'Isn't that right, Grandpa?' she added to the room in general.

'Erm, Grandma. Grandpa isn't actually here right now.'

'Yes, I know!' Grandma said. 'I meant that . . . I meant that . . . Anyway! Enough of that.' Her face clouded over. 'I suppose I should probably start thinking about packing my stuff. I don't have much. Just my pictures and my trophies.' She looked sadly at the photos on the wall.

'No, Grandma! You can't!'

'Sometimes, Greta, it's best to accept things

that you can't change without making a big old song and dance about it. Make the best of the situation. Just like when I had to stop racing cars. I missed the excitement. The thrill. And winning! Oh, how I missed winning. But your grandfather was right – those cars were ever so dangerous. So much safer to pack it in. And –' she sighed – 'maybe Grandpa will come with me to my new home.'

'Yes,' said Greta. 'I'm sure he will.'

Greta had never been more sure in her life that something would not happen.

But then an idea started unfurling in Greta's

mind. Percy might have tried and failed to spook her parents, but perhaps Grandpa Woebegone could succeed . . . ? It would be hard to persuade him, but surely it was worth a try?

'Grandma,' said Greta. 'Do you think Grandpa might help me?

'Of course he would!' said Grandma.

'But . . . how can I put this?' Greta said gently. 'Grandpa is quite . . . grumpy, isn't he?'

Grandma gave Greta a sad smile. 'Yes. He is.'

'In fact, I think he might be the grumpiest person I have ever met.'

Grandma gave a short laugh. 'Me too!'

'But, Grandma . . . if you don't mind me asking . . . he's so grumpy – how did you love him?'

'I still *do* love him, Greta – that doesn't stop after someone dies. Oh, when I first met him, he was dashing and charming and good and kind. But life can take its toll on you. Especially if you live with regret.'

'What sort of regret?'

Grandma sighed. 'Your grandfather was a

very . . . cautious man. He didn't like risks or change. All through his life he always took the safest option and maybe that left him . . . unsatisfied. My old racing car coach always used to say to me, "It's better to regret something you have done, than something you haven't." But your grandpa didn't agree. "Safety first", that was *his* motto.'

Greta nodded. She knew all too well what dangers lurked out in the world.

'Not long after I stopped racing, he was offered a job in New York of all places, to help start a brand-new business. I could tell that part of him wanted to go on this new adventure, but in the end he decided to stay here and keep his safe but boring job. So, at his insistence, we led an uneventful life. Full of love, but quiet. As the years rolled on, I could see the "what ifs" eating away at him. He grew short-tempered. By the end I think he wished he had lived his life differently, but he could never admit it, even to himself.'

'How sad,' said Greta, and Grandma blinked,

as if waking up from a long nap.

'Anyway, listen to me, rattling on. The point is, trust me, if you really need Grandpa, he'll help you. Underneath that gruff exterior he has a heart of gold.'

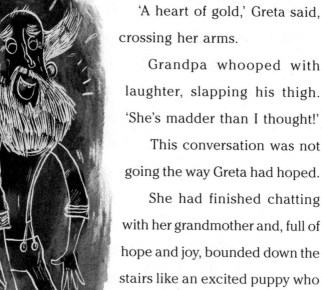

'She said I HAD A WHAT?'

'A heart of gold,' Greta said, crossing her arms.

Grandpa whooped with laughter, slapping his thigh. 'She's madder than I thought!'

This conversation was not going the way Greta had hoped.

She had finished chatting with her grandmother and, full of hope and joy, bounded down the stairs like an excited puppy who had just heard the word 'walkies', and found Grandpa Woebegone and Percy in the sitting room.

'So,' she had said, sitting on

a rug, 'we need to scare my parents more.'

'I knew it!' shouted Percy. 'I knew you didn't think I was spooky enough!'

'No!' said Greta. 'You *are* incredibly spooky . . . But my parents are very difficult to spook.'

'Hmm,' said Percy suspiciously.

'Come on!' roared Grandpa, laughing. 'You're about as spooky as . . . as spooky as . . . Blast it, I can't think of anything! Well, let's just agree that you simply aren't the slightest bit spooky and leave it at that,' Grandpa finished, giving a firm nod.

'And that's why,' Greta said to Grandpa, 'it is *your* turn to help.'

'What?!' asked Grandpa, eyes wide. 'Why on earth do you think *I'd* help?'

'Because Grandma says that underneath all your grumpiness, you have a heart of gold.'

Once Grandpa's laughter had died down, Greta glared at him beadily.

'And anyway, you've been perfectly happy to tell

Percy how *un*spooky he is,' Greta said.

'Well, no, when I said he wasn't spooky, I meant that he *was* spooky, b-but . . .' Grandpa stammered.

'Well, now you've got the chance to show us what you can do. And if you don't . . .' Greta pulled her recorder from her back pocket. 'Let's just say you'll be hearing a lot more of *this* in future. I've been thinking of taking my Grade One actually . . .'

Grandpa gasped. 'What? No! Anything but that! Fine! I'll help!'

'Well, what do you know?' said Greta, grinning. 'Looks like you do have a heart of gold after all.'

Maybe there was more to Greta than I had given her credit for.

'But I'm warning you! If we keep scaring them, it will bring trouble!'

'Grandpa, we *need* to. We have no choice.'

'Yes. So you say. Anyway what do you expect me to do?' Grandpa grumbled. 'I'm not sure my spooking skills are quite what you need. I can't make people see me, and I can't make things move or anything like that. I can't really do anything.'

Percy clapped his hands. 'Forsooth, why don't you possess somebody?' he suggested. 'Now *that's* spooky.'

'"Possess"?' said Greta. 'What's that?'

'Oh, Grandpa Woebegone can jump inside the body of a person and take over their mind.'

'Really? Can you?' asked Greta. 'That would be perfect!'

'Well, I . . . erm . . . I suppose . . .' said Grandpa.

'He can!' said Percy. 'I have seen him do it before!'

'Gah!' snapped Grandpa. 'Yes, I can but it's too risky! Far too dangerous. And I hate doing it.'

'Great!' said Greta, only half listening to her grandfather's protestations. 'You can just possess Mother or Father and –'

'I can't possess adults who don't believe in ghosts,' said Grandpa firmly. 'Their minds are so closed I can't get in.'

'Well, what *can* you possess then?'

'Animals or children,' said Grandpa. 'But before you ask, I am *not* possessing your cat. The last time I did I –'

'You possessed Pussy Lanimous? Why?'

'I was bored. But never again. I still have the fleas.'

'Well, can you possess me?' suggested Greta.

'And then what? Say spooky things? They'll just think you're pretending.'

'Hmm,' said Greta. 'Good point. Then that leaves . . .'

'Your brother!' said Percy.

'Exactly!' said Greta.

'That might just work . . .' said Grandpa.

'Right then! Let's get him!'

Greta sprang up and rushed from the room. A moment later, she came back in, Whats-his-name trailing behind her.

'Hello there!' Greta said to him brightly. 'How are you?'

'Hello, Greta. You like lorry?' said Whats, holding out a shining red lorry.

'Oooh, yes! That's a lovely lorry,' said Greta.

'I want new lorry!'

You see? Absolutely lorry obsessed.

'You want a new lorry?' asked Greta, a cunning look crossing her brow. 'Well, if you help me, I'll buy you a new lorry!'

Bribery? There was *definitely* more to Greta than met the eye.

'Yes! New lorry! Today I did a big curly poo on the potty.'

'Really? That's wonderful news,' said Greta, who seemed overly interested at this new and rather unnecessary information.

Greta turned to Grandpa Woebegone. 'Hang on – in what way is it dangerous?'

'Well, there's a mild muddling of personalities afterwards.'

'That doesn't sound *that* bad –'

'And a risk of permanent personality replacement.'

'WHAT?'

'There is a possibility that your brother's soul will be dissolved forever into nothingness and I will be stuck inside his body forever. It's extremely dangerous really.'

Greta looked at her little brother.

'I want new lorry.'

Greta considered for a moment.

A very, very short moment.

'Let's do it.'

'But . . . but –' spluttered Grandpa.

'Yes, let's do it!'

Greta knew that if they had any chance of spooking her mother and father enough to convince them that ghosts were real, this was the only way.

Grandpa shook his head, then walked over to Whats, who obviously could not see him. He turned to Greta. 'You're *absolutely* sure?'

She nodded gravely at Grandpa.

'Right then. Absolute silence from now on. I need maximum concentration,' said Grandpa. 'Here goes.'

He closed his eyes and started breathing deeply. A few moments later, he started to shimmer and waver, and then, like smoke getting sucked up a chimney, he was drawn forward and into Whats-his-name's left ear.

Whats's eyes opened wide in surprise and he

fell straight on to his back, staring at the ceiling.

Greta stepped over to her little brother, who blinked up at her.

She kneeled down. 'You OK?'

'Yes, I'm fine, you ludicrous child! Now give me a hand up!'

'Is that you, Grandpa?' asked Greta, eyes boggling.

'Of course it is,' said Grandpa Whats-his-name. 'Who the blazes do you think it is?'

Greta was – for once – lost for words.

She pulled her little brother to his feet and watched as he brushed himself down.

'I *hate* being this small,' he grumbled. 'And, ugh, for goodness' sake, his nappy is wet! Can I get a fresh nappy please? This really is intolerable.'

Percy burst out laughing. 'Oh, now *that* is funny!'

'Be quiet, boy!' said Grandpa Whats-his-name.

'Look,' said Greta, snapping out of her daze, 'I'm not changing you, so let's just get on with this as quickly as possible, OK?'

Grandpa Whats-his-name glared at Greta.

'Fine. Get your parents in and let's get this over with. Before this nappy starts giving me a rash.'

Greta went to the door and yelled, 'Mother! Father! Come here! There's something wrong with Larry!'

Of course! The child's name is *Larry*! How could I forget?

Very easily, in fact, because it is a very forgettable name. I *much* prefer Whats. I mean – who even calls a child 'Larry'?

Grandpa Larry Whats-his-name lay back on the floor, stuck his tongue out of the side of his mouth, opened his eyes wide and started groaning loudly.

'Quickly!' shouted Greta.

Her father wheeled in first, followed by her mother.

'What is it?' asked William Woebegone. 'What's all the shouting about?'

'Yes! You know this is my meditation hour!' Prosecca snapped. 'I'll never get my mind back in the relaxation zone!'

'But look!' Greta pointed to Grandpa Larry Whats-his-name, who was now rolling around on the floor. 'There's something wrong with Larry!'

Greta's mother put her hands on her hips. 'Oh, for goodness' sake! Has he lost his lorry again?'

'I don't think so,' said Greta. 'I think it might be something . . . spooky.'

Grandpa Larry Whats-his-name started groaning again.

'Get up off the floor, Larry! You're making the carpet dirty!' Greta's mother said.

Grandpa Larry Whats-his-name gave another groan.

'And stop that racket! It's giving off dreadful vibrations.' She turned to her husband. 'I don't know what is up with that child.'

'Looks like constipation to me,' he replied, giving her a knowledgeable nod. 'Used to get it myself when I was his age. Some prunes will sort him out.'

Grandpa Larry Whats-his-name gave another terrible groan. He opened one eye, and the other. Then, arms rigid out in front of him, he floated up on to his feet. That actually was rather spooky, but Greta's parents were so busy discussing their son's toilet habits, they missed it completely.

'Look at that!' cried Greta, too late.

Her parents turned to see Greta pointing at the now-standing Grandpa Larry Whats-his-name and looked suitably unimpressed.

'Very good,' Greta's mother said. 'Now toddle off and play with your lorries.'

Grandpa Larry Whats-his-name raised one arm in the air and pointed a finger at his mother.

'I do not wish to play with my lorries, foolish lady!' he boomed in a voice that rattled the dusty chandeliers.

'Don't call your mother that!' Greta's father said. 'You know she thinks the word "lady" makes her

sound old.' He pointed his pipe at Grandpa Larry Whats-his-name. 'And I won't have you using that tone of voice inside my house.'

'Thank you, darling. I don't know where he gets such ill manners from,' Greta's mother said, shaking her head.

'I told you all that positive parenting nonsense was a waste of time,' Greta's father replied.

Greta's mother ignored her husband and turned to Grandpa Larry Whats-his-name. 'If you don't want to play with your lorries, go and find something else to play with then.'

'Imbeciles! I do not wish to play! For I come bearing a message!' Grandpa Larry Whats-his-name boomed.

'Don't call your father an imbecile!' Greta's mother snapped.

'I think he might have called us *both* imbeciles, darling,' Greta's father replied. 'And where did you learn the word "imbecile" anyway?'

It should be mentioned that at this point William Woebegone was talking to both his son *and* his own father at the same time. It was all very confusing.

'And anyway – what message?' Greta's father continued.

Grandpa Larry Whats-his-name stood up to his tallest height (which wasn't very tall because he was only three) and drew a deep breath. 'I come bearing tidings . . . from the other side! And also to ask for a fresh nappy, for I am getting rather rashy.'

'What *is* the child blathering on about?' Greta's father asked, turning to his wife, who shrugged. '*What* message? *What* other side?'

'THE other side!' exploded Grandpa Larry Whats-his-name. 'The unearthly realm where spirits roam free!'

'I have to admit,' Greta's mother said, 'I'm delighted with his vocabulary progress. So advanced for a three-year-old! Playing all those audiobooks to him when I was pregnant has really paid off.'

Grandpa Larry Whats-his-name huffed. 'Silence! I am not of this world. I am a spirit!'

'You're nothing of the sort! You're a very naughty boy with a big soggy nappy,' said Greta's mother.

'Now, let's go and change you before you get any grumpier.'

'I am a ghost!' shouted Grandpa Larry Whats-his-name. 'And I have possessed the body of your child!'

Prosecca Woebegone turned to Greta. 'Did you put him up to this?'

Greta gasped. 'What? No! I –'

'You've been going on and on about ghosts recently, telling us they exist, and now you've taught your brother all these fancy words to try to prove it, haven't you? Well, I'm on to you, young lady!'

'OH FOR GOODNESS' SAKE!' groaned Grandpa Larry Whats-his-name, putting his head in his hands. 'Ghosts do exist! You have one inside your son right now!'

'I have just about had enough of this nonsense,' snapped Greta's mother. 'It's nappy-change time!'

She strode over, bent down and picked up Grandpa Larry Whats-his-name.

'What? No!' cried Grandpa Larry Whats-his-name,

pummelling her with his tiny fists. 'No! Wait until I have left the child's body! PUT ME DOWN, WOMAN! PUT ME DOWN THIS INSTANT!'

'No, young man! It's nappy-change time and there's nothing you can do about it!' she said, and carried the wailing Grandpa Larry Whats-his-name out of the room.

'Now,' said Greta's father, turning to Greta, 'I want no more of this ghost nonsense, young lady.'

And with that he wheeled out of the room, leaving Greta and Percy in stunned silence.

'Alas,' Percy said. 'That did not go very well. At all.'

Greta could not muster a reply.

'They didn't seem in the slightest bit spooked,' continued Percy.

'No,' Greta conceded. 'They did not.'

And that meant that their plan had failed *again*. There was no convincing her parents that ghosts really did exist.

A few minutes later, Greta's mother deposited Grandpa Larry Whats-his-name back in the sitting room.

'Now you two BE QUIET,' she snarled. 'Mummy will be upstairs meditating.'

And off she flounced, leaving a very embarrassed-looking Grandpa Larry Whats-his-name stood in his new nappy.

'I don't want this ever spoken about again,' he said after a moment. 'Or there'll be big trouble. Agreed?'

Percy and Greta both nodded.

Grandpa Larry Whats-his-name closed his eyes and breathed deeply. A few long, slow breaths later, a shimmering, swirling smoky Grandpa drifted out of the body of Larry Whats-his-name, who promptly fell on to his bum.

Greta gave Grandpa Woebegone a sad smile. 'Never mind,' she said gently. 'Thank you for trying.'

Grandpa Woebegone gave her a sad smile back, and then said softly:

'Where my lorry?'

CHAPTER 9

Fortunately for Grandpa Woebegone and Larry Whats-his-name, it did not take long for them to return to normal. Larry once again became the lorry-obsessed three-year-old, and Grandpa Woebegone resumed being a very old, grumpy ghost – now even grumpier because of a spot of nappy rash. Greta, however, normally a relentlessly positive child, was struggling to pick herself up from the gloom caused by the total failure to spook her parents.

This was made much, much worse the next day.

Her parents had been out all morning and come back in before lunch bubbling with excitement. Greta only found out why as she was gnawing

on a cheese and pickle baguette.

'It really is lovely, darling,' Greta's mother said
to her husband, nibbling at some avocado. 'It's
definitely the right place!'

'What?' said Greta, stopping chewing.

'Don't speak with your mouth full, Greta darling,'
her mother said.

'What did you say?' Greta said, ignoring her.

'I said, don't speak with your mouth full! Is there something wrong with your hearing?'

Greta swallowed both the half-chewed baguette and her frustration. 'What did you say *before*? What's "lovely" and "definitely the right place"?'

'Well,' Greta's mother said, sharing a knowing glance with her husband before returning Greta's gaze and smiling, 'we have found the perfect care home for your grandmother! Isn't that the most wonderful news?'

'NO! It is NOT the most wonderful news!' shouted Greta.

'Now, Greta. St Atilla's really is a smashing place,' said her father. 'It has a fountain right outside her front door. They pump a chemical scent throughout the whole building, so it smells of roses instead of old people. And they play bingo on Fridays. And rugby on Tuesdays. I mean, it's a bit slow but –'

'Grandma hates bingo! And she can hardly walk, so I can't imagine she'll be playing much rugby!'

'And it's not far away,' continued her father. 'You'll be able to visit her at least once a month.'

Greta gasped. 'Once a *month*?'

'Yes! And the best thing,' Greta's mother trilled, 'is that they have a room available *right now*. She'll be out – I mean, *in* – by the end of the week!'

'WHAT?!' shouted Greta. 'YOU CAN'T!'

'We can. And we will,' said her mother. 'She can't possibly look after herself or her money any more.'

'It's for the best, love,' said Greta's father.

'You've no idea what's best for her!'

'We all know she's not getting any better. You know. Up there.' Greta's father tapped the side of his head meaningfully. 'And we aren't going to let her behaviour upset you any more.'

'She doesn't upset me! You don't understand! You pretend to care, but you don't! You don't listen. I'm TELLING you that there *are* ghosts in this house and *you* just don't see them!'

'Now that's enough of that ghost talk!' roared her father. 'I won't have it!'

'For your sake we can't leave it any longer,' Greta's mother said to Greta, then she turned to

her husband. 'Every day it gets worse and worse.'
She pointed upstairs. 'She leaves *tomorrow*.'

'No!' cried Greta. 'You just want her out of the
house so you can turn her bedroom into a stupid
yoga studio! Well, that's not very . . . yogic!'

Greta slammed the rest of the baguette down
on her plate and ran out of the room.

'How *dare* you tell me I'm not very yogic!' Greta's
mother shouted after her fast-disappearing daughter.
'I'm very yogic!' She turned to her husband and gave
him a look of utter fury. 'That girl is completely
destroying my psychic balance!'

Greta was doing her best to put on a brave face as
she helped her grandmother pack her belongings
into an old leather suitcase. Her face was still red
and blotchy from a tedious bout of crying, the details
of which I will not bore you with. But, believe me,
it was *never-ending*.

She was filling the suitcase with Grandma's
nighties and cardigans, her dressing gown, her
trophies, and the other little knick-knacks that

gathered dust on the top of her wardrobe and on the windowsill – little crystal animals, old jewellery, a small clay plate Greta had made her for her birthday, a wedding photo of her and Grandpa Woebegone. You get the idea – all sorts of worthless junk.

Greta looked at the wedding photo, which was housed in an ancient leather picture frame. Grandma was beaming in a white dress and veil. Greta had to admit, Grandpa Woebegone looked rather dashing in his wedding suit.

'He was so handsome.' Grandma nodded at the photo. 'And so exciting! Such a whirlwind romance. And he adored me. That's why he said I had to give up the racing. He loved me so much – he couldn't bear the thought of losing me.'

Grandma sighed. 'I do miss him. I mean, obviously I still talk to him, so that's nice,' she added quickly. 'But it's not the same.'

Silence blanketed the room like snow at night. Greta knew not to say anything – but she went over and hugged her grandmother, who felt small and fragile in her arms.

'Are you sure you should be hugging the witch?'

'HOW LONG HAVE YOU BEEN THERE?' Greta shouted, turning to see Percy staring at them.

'Not long,' Percy said. 'But you should be careful. At the very least she'll give you warts. And at worst she might eat you.'

'MY GRANDMA WILL NOT EAT ME!'

'Pardon?' said Grandma.

'But witches eat children all the time!' said Percy.

'For the *last* time my grandma is NOT a witch,' growled Greta.

'Thank you, dear,' said Grandma. 'That's very kind of you to say.'

'You,' Greta said, pointing at Percy. 'Out of here. Now!'

Percy gave her a nervous grin and slowly backed out of the door, closely followed by a fuming Greta. 'Follow me!' she snapped.

A moment later, she closed the door of her bedroom behind them.

'You have to stop calling my grandma a witch!' she scolded Percy.

Percy looked nervously at the floor. 'I'm sorry, but when I'm from –'

'Whenever you're from, you aren't there now! Times have changed. We don't have witches any more. And we don't push pieces of poo around with a stick for fun either!'

'Well, maybe you should try it!'

'I don't want to try it!'

This was a lie; only the day before, Greta had spent a very pleasant half an hour playing a few rounds of Stick-Push-a-Poo with something left on the landing by Pussy Lanimous.

'I'm just saying,' Greta continued, 'you need to accept that the world is different now.'

Percy looked crestfallen. 'It's not easy, you know.'

After a moment, Greta's face softened and she said gently, 'What's it actually like? Being a gho– Being a no-body, I mean?'

Percy thought for a moment. 'It's very lonely. When the last person who knew you dies, nobody remembers you any more, and it's like you never existed. The world forgets you. And you feel . . . useless.' Percy sniffled. 'Like, what was the point of me? My life was so meaningless.'

Greta couldn't help but think of her grandmother, the memories of her racing career fading over the years.

Percy looked out of the window. 'I've always thought that graveyard is so beautiful,' he said.

'Really?' Greta replied. 'I think it's a bit sad. And strange – seeing so many of my family buried there.'

'No,' said Percy. 'All those people were loved. And never forgotten. It must be so good to be . . . remembered,' he said in a quiet voice. 'To be marked like that.'

'I won't forget you, Percy,' said Greta, eyes watering. 'Ever.'

Percy gave Greta a wide grin through his tears. 'Thank you,' he croaked.

And then the most extraordinary thing happened.

So extraordinary Greta wasn't sure at first if she had imagined it. But it was almost as if Percy *faded*. As if he became the tiniest bit more see-through. She rubbed her eyes. He was still very much there, but definitely a tiny bit *less* there.

And at that very moment the tiniest kernel of an idea began to sprout in Greta's tiny mind . . . an idea that might just help the numbskull Percy Woebegone.

But before it could grow it was interrupted by

the appearance of Grandpa Woebegone.

'What are you two snivelling about?'

'We are not snivelling!' Greta shouted, wiping her face with the back of her sleeve.

This was Greta's second lie in as many minutes.

'Anyway,' said Greta. 'Even if I am upset, what's wrong with that? I'm losing my grandma and best friend, and there's nothing wrong with being sad about *that*! Maybe what's wrong is that *you* aren't sad about her going.'

'I see no point in getting all emotional about things!' said Grandpa. 'In my day we didn't get upset all the time. Stiff upper lips, that's what we had. We just picked ourselves up, dusted ourselves down and moved on. Doesn't do any good to dwell on things. No time for regret or sadness. Crying is weakness!'

Greta gasped. 'Crying is not weakness! That's nonsense. It's OK to be sad, Grandpa.'

'Balderdash!'

Greta had absolutely no idea what balderdash was, but it did not sound very nice.

'I don't think dashing balls is going to help

anybody,' she said. 'I think you need to be sad. Grandma is going and that is sad.'

'Poppycock!' shouted Grandpa. 'Pack your troubles away and don't think about 'em. That's the ticket!'

Greta also had no idea what poppycock was, but it didn't sound nice either.

'Perhaps it's better for her anyway,' Grandpa Woebegone said with a little more gentleness in his voice than usual. 'Safer without all these stairs. They'll take care of her there. And there's nothing we can do anyway. We tried to stop it. Twice. And we failed twice. We did our best and that's all we can do.'

He's right, Greta thought glumly.

Two ghosts had tried to spook her parents.

Two ghosts had totally failed to spook her parents.

And that meant Grandma was moving out tomorrow.

She had failed.

But then Greta remembered something.

Or *someone* rather.

Her eyes lit up. 'Maybe there's still a way . . .'

'What do you mean?' asked Percy.

'Grandpa,' Greta said, excitement growing in her voice, 'didn't you say there were *three* ghosts in this house?'

'Yes, but –'

'That means a third chance. I think I need to talk to this other ghost.'

Percy and Grandpa both gasped at the same time.

'No!'

'NO, YOU CANNOT, GRETA! NOT THAT RAKISH RAMPALLIAN!' shouted Percy.

'Yes, I can.'

'Well, you can, but you shouldn't,' said Grandpa. 'It's . . . not safe.'

'What do you mean "not safe"?' asked Greta.

'He's dangerous,' wailed Percy.

'Poppydash!' said Greta. 'Baldercock! He can't be *that* bad!'

'He is,' whimpered Percy. 'He's evil!'

'A real rotten egg,' agreed Grandpa. 'Completely

barmy on the crumpet.'

'Barmy on the *what*? Actually, don't bother answering. It doesn't matter.'

'Please,' said Percy. 'He's –'

Greta held her hand up. 'I'm afraid my mind is made up. I'm going to meet this other ghost. And I'm going to ask him for help.' She stood, the look of grim determination on her face matched by the fear on Percy and Grandpa's. 'I'm going to the cellar.'

And with that Greta Woebegone marched down from her room, down the stairs and down to the cellar.

Where, finally, *I* shall make my entrance.

CHAPTER
10

'Thank goodness,' I hear you say, dear reader. 'Now *you* are here, finally this book will get interesting.'

And could I argue with that?

I could not.

But first it is time to let you know a little about myself.

It is not a happy tale, truth be told, but which interesting stories are?

My name is Wolfgang van Bach-Storey. I was born in 1802 in a small village in the Duchy of Württemberg called Smackenzibotten. Even before I was born, my parents could tell I was a musical prodigy; my mother had accidentally swallowed a pair of silver spoons while pregnant, and soon they could hear from her stomach the unmistakable sound of me playing merry little jigs on them.

When I was two, my parents sent me away to a musical tutor in the nearby town of Slappenzeebum. When I was six, my parents sent me away to the esteemed music school in München. When I was nine, my parents sent me away to learn with the masters at the university in Vienna. When I was twelve, my parents just sent me away, saying they had rented my room out to a young mackerel merchant called Hans Unveet, and I finally got the message. They were jealous of my talent.

So I packed my meagre belongings, left the family home for the last time and made my way across Europe, earning my keep by playing the harpsichord in beer houses. I finally arrived on the cobbled streets of London, my back near broken from carrying the harpsichord across the breadth of the continent.

It was in that great city that I at last made my fortune. I played my way up from the dirty bars of

the City of London to the great houses of the well-to-do, glittering concert halls and then, eventually, to the vast palace of Buckingham, where I had the immense honour to play before Her Esteemed Majesty Queen Victoria.

It was there and then, though, when my fame was at its highest, when my star had risen to its peak, that I came crashing to earth and all my dreams turned to dust.

It was to be the greatest moment of my career. I was invited to perform for the queen at her birthday celebrations. Everything had to be *perfect*. I had my best clothes washed and dried, and powdered my finest wig. I was ready in plenty of time, and before arriving at the palace, I stopped at a favourite little restaurant and had a modest dinner of a dozen fresh oysters, German sausage, potato goulash, Wiener schnitzel and sauerkraut, followed by Viennese apfelstrudel and creamy käsespätzle, and some fine chocolates from Belgium, all washed down with a little beer. And some French wine. And some schnapps. And coffee with a dash of brandy.

Replete and satisfied, I set out to meet my destiny. As I approached Buckingham Palace, my horse-drawn carriage rattled and jiggled on the cobblestones, and it was there that my problems began.

A great disturbance started to grow in my belly, like a foul storm gathering on the horizon.

I forced it to the back of my mind, though, as we arrived at the gates. Having loosened my belt and a button or two on my shirt to relive the strain placed upon them, I was ready to make my entrance.

I stumbled slightly out of the carriage, my nerves

getting the better of me. I took my place by the harpsichord in the ballroom as we waited for the queen to make her entrance.

Lords and ladies took their seats, their jewellery twinkling in the light of the myriad candles that lit the room. A hush fell upon the expectant audience, only disturbed by a sudden and enormous gurgling from my stomach. It was like the rolling rumble of thunder on a dark night. It echoed around the silent room, causing the lords and ladies to turn to see from where – and from *whom* – the noise had come.

I kept my head down and prayed that that would be the end of my digestive misfortune. Sweat prickled my forehead and trickled down my back.

However, the strain on my stomach became more intense, and I was forced to release another notch on my belt.

At once everyone stood and, with a great trumpet blast, the queen entered the hall.

Alas, it was not to be the only great trumpet blast of the evening.

The queen took her seat on a great golden chair, and the soft chattering murmur from the audience once more gave way to weighty silence.

It was my moment.

I took a breath and swallowed, my throat suddenly dry.

I stared at the music on the sheets in front of me, but the notes swam before my eyes. No matter; I knew the piece by heart.

I placed my fingers on the harpsichord, ready to begin.

I took a deep breath. A mistake, as it happens.

The deep growling in my stomach rose into an unstoppable wind, which tore through me, until it exited my rear end at high speed as an ear-splitting, room-shaking fart.

The foul stench was immediate and terrible, but worse – so much worse! – was the fact that the blast from my bottom directed itself towards an ill-placed candle on a small table behind me.

Calamity! The gassy fart hit the candle and erupted into a blast of fire of great length and heat.

And woe upon woe! The great flaming fart touched a velvet curtain, which immediately caught fire.

Chaos broke out. Gasps of terror filled the hall as the flames began to spread. The pale-faced queen was ushered out, quickly followed by the screaming audience.

I stood in horror as servants pulled down the curtain and doused it with buckets of water until finally the fire, like my career, was snuffed out.

I was shoved forcefully by rough hands out of the ballroom, out of the palace, and on to the pavement.

It was the last time I was ever to set foot in a palace, and my hands never touched a musical instrument again. My descent from high society was swift and hard. I could no longer get employment as a musician anywhere; I was banished from the great houses to the lowliest taverns. My name was mud. Wherever I went, I was known as the man who had farted in front of the queen and nearly destroyed Buckingham Palace.

Forced out of my home, I wandered the streets, dirty, hungry and unloved. I cursed the day I had ever left Smackenzibotten. I wailed at my cruel, underserved fate. The great and eminent musician Wolfgang van Bach-Storey left starving in a gutter, merely because of one unfortunate bottom fizzle, which was absolutely no fault of my own! The more I pondered my unlucky fate, the angrier and more hateful towards the world I became.

At last I found work as a worm farmer, making a mere shilling per hundred worms. Me! A lowly worm farmer! My delicate fingers bespattered with muck and accidentally squished worms!

And one winter's day, as I dug for worms in the bitter wet and cold, kneeling on the frozen earth, the wind whipping across the field, I swore I would get revenge on the world that had treated me so poorly.

On the way home

that night to my lodgings in the very house where the Woebegone family now resides, I stopped for one or two pints of beer to celebrate my new plan for revenge. It was the unfortunate final note in my life that, later that night, having had no more than three, or maybe four, pints of beer, perhaps a little gin, some whiskies and a bottle of wine, as I clambered down the stairs to my bedroom in the dank cellar of the house, my foot slipped, and I tumbled and broke my neck.

I was dead. And I awoke as a ghost.

And that is my story. I warned you it was not a happy tale. I am sure you now understand my anger and bitterness – and my thirst for revenge. I am sure you see why I have spent my time – hundreds of years – in the cellar in this house, plotting and planning, the hatred in my heart festering like the mould that grew in the darkest corners of my home.

And then, with a bounce in her step, hopeful young Greta Woebegone skipped down the stairs into my lair . . .

'Hello,' Greta whispered into the dark, the fear in her voice so thick I could almost taste it. 'Hello, Mr Ghost? Is there anybody here?'

Greta flicked on the light switch. One bare light bulb swung, casting shadows that jumped around the cellar. A furry shape skittered under a cupboard. It was Ludwig, my pet rat and only friend in this cruel, cruel world.

'Hello, little Ludwig!' I whispered and waved to him.

He raised a tiny paw in greeting. 'Hello,' Ludwig squeaked. 'It's not healthy that you are talking to a rat, you know. In fact, it's rather pathetic.'

'You are so funny, my furry little friend!'

Ludwig shook his tiny head, gave me one final look – of love, I think – and scuttled off into the dark.

Greta swung round towards me. 'Who was that?' she gasped,

peering into the gloom to see where the voice had come from.

It was time to reveal myself.

'Hello, Greta . . .' I whispered by her ear.

Greta spun round. 'How do you know my name?'

'I can slip into your mind and read your thoughts like notes of music on a page,' I whispered.

'Well, don't,' she said. 'It's rude. And stop whispering.'

'I am not whispering,' I whispered. 'My words crawl inside your mind like maggots, feeding on your –'

'Your words are not crawling inside my mind like maggots, thank you very much! You are whispering because you think it makes you sound creepy. Well, it doesn't. So stop it.'

I remained silent, a little annoyed at *her* rudeness. My whispering was *definitely* creepy.

It was time to teach the girl some manners.

'You dare come down here, *child*,' I whispered. 'When I –'

'If you don't stop this whispering nonsense,

I shall go straight back upstairs.'

'Well, maybe I *shall* speak at a normal volume then,' I said, thinking I had done enough creepy whispering for one day. 'Maybe it is too terrifying for you . . .'

I ran a fingernail across her cheek, leaving a thin line of ectoplasm like a slug trail.

'Ugh, *what* is that?' she said, wiping her face.

'It's ectoplasm. A spiritual slime I can produce.'

'Well, don't! It's disgusting. And I really will leave if you do that again.'

'Ah, but you won't,' I said. 'Because you need my help, don't you?'

'How do you know?'

'I already told you. I can slip into your mind and read your thoughts like –'

'Yes, like notes of music on a page. OK – so you'll help?' asked Greta.

'I will not, foolish girl. For it is time,' I said, 'to reveal myself!'

I finally slowly began to appear in front of her in all my hideous glory.

She gasped once again. I could smell her fear.

I grew in height, towering over her. 'It is time to EAT YOUR SOUL!'

I could see the terror in her eyes, as she stared at me in horror and –

'Oh, do give over,' she said, yawning. Yawning! How dare she?! 'You aren't going to be eating any souls. And you're going to have to do an awful lot better than that if you're going to scare my parents.'

Such a rude and impolite girl.

'Now,' Greta continued, 'maybe you can start by telling me your name?'

'My name is Wolfgang van Bach-Storey,' I said.

'Pardon? Did you say your name is Wolfgang van *Bach-Storey*?'

'*Ja*. That is my name. Why are you smirking?'

'I'm not smirking!'

The light was dim but I could see she was *totally* smirking.

'OK,' she continued, 'and how did you end up as a ghost in this house?'

I sighed. 'It is not a happy tale,' I began. 'I was born in a small village called Smackenzibotten in the Duchy of Württemberg in 1802. Even before I was born –'

'Sorry, you were born *where*?'

'I was born in Smackenzibotten. Why are you giggling?'

'I'm not giggling!' Greta said. 'It was coughing!'

'Does my story amuse you? Because I will not continue if –'

'No! I'm sorry,' she said, wiping her eyes. 'Please continue.'

And so I told her my tragic story, only pausing when she started coughing again as I told her about my being sent away to Slappenzeebum.

Once I reached the end of my terrible tale, she wiped her eyes again with the back of her hands.

'Oh, dearie me! That was hilariou– tragic, I mean. Poor you!' she said, smiling.

I glared at her. 'Why are you smiling?'

'It's a smile of pity,' she answered quickly.

Is there such a thing as a smile of pity? I wondered.

But before I had time to wonder further, she continued talking.

'And now you want to exact revenge on everybody because of your miserable life?'

'*Ja*. I do. Very much,' I said. Because I really did.

'Well, that's perfect!' she said, clapping her hands. 'You can take your revenge out on my parents and really terrify them!'

'And why shouldn't I take my revenge on you, child?' I asked perfectly reasonably.

'Because,' she said. 'Because . . . ermmmm . . .'

'You don't know, do you?

'I do know!'

She did not know.

'Just give me a moment,' she continued, her mind flapping like a dying mackerel in the bottom of a boat. 'Becauuuuuuse . . . Oh! Yes! I know! Because you and I are both musical souls. You with your harpsichord; me with my recorder. And my parents are always trying to get me to stop playing the recorder, just like society stopped you from playing your harpsichord. Our story is very similar, if you think about it.'

She was clever. Very clever. But she failed to realize I had actually heard her play the recorder, which was perhaps the worst torture for a true musical soul like mine. But I could not stand by and watch another person's musical dreams – however ludicrous and misplaced – be crushed by miserable parents, like mine had been centuries before.

I made up my mind. 'I shall help you, Greta Woebegone,' I declared. 'I will terrify your parents until they do little widdles in their pants!'

'Brilliant!' she said, clapping her hands. 'I will call a ghost meeting!'

'I'm not coming to a ghost meeting,' said Percy. 'Not with . . . him,' he added, pointing towards the cellar.

The foolish boy did not even realize I was not

always in the cellar. He did not know I could move throughout the house, silent and invisible, spying.

No, not spying. *Observing.* I could see everything.

'He's not that bad,' said Greta.

'I'm not sure,' said Grandpa Woebegone. 'Always seemed like a very rum sort to me. Far too dangerous!'

'The last time I spoke to him, he threatened to eat my soul!' Percy wailed.

It's true. I did. And his reaction *was* very funny.

'He's not going to do anything like that. He's actually rather . . . sweet once you get to know him a bit.'

Sweet?! How dare she?

Eventually Greta managed to persuade the cowardly pair of ghosts to come to my lair.

They shuffled down the stairs, Percy hiding behind Grandpa Woebegone, who was hiding behind Greta. I followed at the rear.

At the foot of the stairs they

paused to look for me. I could sense their fear. I waited until I could feel their nerves were completely shredded and then revealed myself.

'Tremble before me,' I whispered to the cowering trio. 'For I am evil incarn–'

'Great, now we're all here,' Greta interrupted rather rudely. 'I called this meeting so we can all put our heads together and work out how to truly terrify my parents.'

'I'm not doing anything to help,' said Grandpa Woebegone, pointing at me, 'until he apologizes for being so blasted horrible.'

'I'm not apologizing!' I said. 'It's who I am! Why should I be sorry for being who I am?'

'Well, maybe you should think about changing,' Percy bleated. 'You've scared us rotten for years!'

'No! No apologies from me,' I said, and folded my arms to show I meant business.

'Fine!' Grandpa Woebegone said, also folding his arms to show he meant business. 'Well, I'm not going to stand around –'

'OI!' blasted Greta. 'In case you've forgotten we

138

have a job to do here. You are three ghosts and it's time to stop arguing and start haunting! Now, what ideas do you have?'

'I can slip into their minds, and read their thoughts like notes of music on a page . . .' I suggested in a whispery voice.

'That's quite good, maybe useful, but not *particularly* scary,' Greta said. 'Any other ideas?'

'I know,' said Percy. 'I know what *he* can do.' He nodded at me.

'What?' asked Greta breathlessly.

'He has the power to be a poltergeist.'

CHAPTER
11

I t was true. I did have the power to be a poltergeist.

'Now *that*,' said Greta, 'is perfect.'

Now, in case there are any children reading this book – and there really shouldn't be, because children should not be reading stories about ghosts, but if there are – I should explain what a poltergeist is.

A poltergeist is a type of ghost that can interact with the physical world. It can make loud noises, such as knocking on doors and that sort of thing. It can move objects and make them float. It can even pinch and bite and trip people. *So much fun!* I had not used my power in so long that I had quite forgotten about it.

'The boy with the foul boils is correct. I can indeed be a poltergeist,' I said.

'Wolfgang! Don't be so rude about Percy!' Greta scolded.

'I care not,' said Percy, shrugging. 'In sooth, my boils *are* quite foul.'

'That is the problem with people today,' I said to Percy. 'People are afraid to call somebody with foul boils a foul –'

'That's because it is not nice to draw attention to things like that!' Greta snapped. Then she continued, her voice softer and full of care. 'You should be kind and try to think of other people's feelings. I believe that you can be a better person, Wolfgang. I can see inside your heart, and I see goodness there.' She gave me a warm smile, eyes shining with hope.

I squatted down so I was face to face with her. 'Oh, Greta. If I could give you one thing in life, dear child, I would give you the ability to see yourself through my eyes. Only then would you truly realize what a dreadful goody two shoes you are.'

Greta gasped, no doubt reeling in shock at the truth of my words.

Little Ludwig suddenly scurried past and I grabbed him. 'Isn't that right, my sweet little Ludwig? Isn't she a goody two shoes?' And I gave him a little kiss on the snout. He gave me a kiss back – well, it was more of a bite, actually, but I am sure he meant it affectionately.

Once I had managed to prise him off my lip, I continued. 'You know,' I said to Greta, placing my hand on my chest. 'Your little speech about goodness nearly touched my heart. Not really. I lied. My heart is nothing but a shrivelled black lump.'

Greta glared at me. 'Just be quiet,' she said. 'And start to practise your poltergeisting.'

'Greta, it's too dangerous! Trusting *this* . . . this thing,' Grandpa said, pointing at me, which was rather rude, I think. 'And poltergeisting? Mark my words, no good will come of it!' he grumbled darkly.

'Don't be such a Gloomy Gustav!' I said. 'It will be fine.'

Sadly I was not completely correct in this statement. I was, in fact rather wrong and it was not fine.

In fact, Greta got to see my poltergeisting skills quicker than any of us had expected. She came rushing into the cellar to find me later that very afternoon.

'You have to do the poltergeisting today!' she said desperately.

'Impossible! I am not some performing monkey. I need to prepare myself. Build up my energies.'

'You HAVE to,' said Greta urgently, tears in her eyes. 'I heard my parents talking. They're taking Grandma to the home tomorrow morning!'

I knew this already, of course, but it was fun watching the panic in her eyes. I could sense her deeper fear too – if Grandma was taken away to a new home, Greta would have to leave the house if she wanted to visit her. I could feel her palms sweating at the very thought, her head feeling faint . . .

We decided it would be best to wait for the whole family to be together before I used my supernatural skills.

It was after dinner, and the Woebegone family were all in the sitting room. The sitting room was my least favourite room of the house and I tried to avoid it as far as I could. If I can be honest, it filled me with fear.

And why might I, terrifying ghost that I am, be afraid? Excellent question, thoughtful reader.

It was because in the corner of the room, crouched like a tiger ready to pounce, was a piano. And, oh, how that piano mocked me! Every time I saw it my heart started pounding as my memory returned once again to that night at the palace, and my great shame and fall from society. I loathed being in the same room as it.

And yet . . . the piano also called to me. How I longed to place my fingers on the keys and let the music flow through me again . . .

But no! Music had betrayed me and was buried deep in my past. I tore my eyes from the piano and concentrated on the task at hand.

Greta's father was puffing on his pipe and tapping on a typewriter, working on his latest collection of poetry: *Now That's What I Call a Limerick – Volume 26*. The cat, Pussy Lanimous, was curled up in his lap, purring. Greta's mother was practising yoga on a mat in the middle of the room. Larry Whats-his-name was predictably playing with a lorry in front of the crackling fire.

In short, it was a picture-perfect family scene. Ripe to be spoiled with a healthy dose of terror.

Delicious.

Greta peeked in through a crack in the door.

'Right,' she whispered. 'They're ready. I'm going

to go in, sit down on the sofa and then, a couple of minutes later, you start poltergeisting, OK?'

I nodded. I did not need the plan repeated to me. We had been through it enough times already.

I was ready. I licked my lips.

Greta strolled into the sitting room, and Percy, Grandpa Woebegone and I drifted in behind her. She planted herself on the sofa and pretended to read a comic.

'Darling,' Greta's father said to his wife who was busy performing a downward dog. 'Can you think of a rhyme for "chilly"?'

'Hmm?' Greta's mother murmured.

'Listen. I have:

There was a young man from Caerphilly

Whose hands were incredibly chilly.

To unfreeze them perchance

He stuck his hands down his pants,

But instead felt a little . . .'

'Silly?'

'"Silly!" Perfect, darling!'

'Now please don't interrupt me again,' Prosecca said. 'I'm feeling very trance-like,' she added, sitting with her legs twisted like spaghetti and beginning to chant. 'Ommmmmmmmm . . . Ommmmmm . . .'

Greta looked at me and mouthed: *Now!*

I closed my eyes and breathed in. I could feel the air vibrating around me. I could feel the power coursing through me.

I lifted my arms and the pictures on the walls began to rattle slightly.

It was happening.

'Look at the pictures!' Greta shouted, letting out a loud gasp and pointing at the wall.

147

'Shh!' said her mother. 'Mummy is channelling her chakras.'

The pictures began to rattle more, and the hands of the grandfather clock in the corner began to move backwards.

Greta's father looked up, peering over his spectacles, but then shook his head and went back to typing.

Greta mouthed at me: *More!*

I breathed in more energy and threw it all back out into the room. A cup and saucer began trembling, then fell straight off the table, spilling tea on the carpet.

I flicked the television on and Larry waddled over. He put his hands on the screen, which was flickering with white static, illuminating the room in fluttering light. He turned his head, looking over his shoulder.

'They're here . . .' he whispered.

'Who's here, poppet?' Greta's mother asked

without opening her eyes.

'The lorries . . .' Larry said.

Unbelievable. Absolutely obsessed.

I could feel the wind of psychic energy still building, flowing about the room around and around.

And then Greta's mother began floating.

It was just a little at first, a centimetre or so, but she was slowly getting higher and higher.

Greta's mouth flopped open, followed by Greta's mother's eyes, and she let out a yelp.

'Darling!' she screamed at her husband. 'I'm floating!'

Greta's father's eyes were as wide as saucers. 'I don't believe it!'

Pussy Lanimous was staring at Greta's mother, all his hair on end.

'It must be all the chakra energy I've built up!' exclaimed Prosecca gleefully. 'I knew I could do it!'

'It's not your chakras, Mother!' shouted Greta. 'It's the ghost!'

'Wheeee!' squealed Greta's mother as she twirled in mid-air. 'I can feel the earth energies flowing through me!'

It wasn't working. I needed more power. Unbelievably, and much to my shame, I needed the other ghosts.

'Quickly,' I urged Percy and Grandpa Woebegone, 'we must bring our spirit energy together!'

'Absolutely not!' barked Grandpa Woebegone. 'You didn't let me out for nearly a decade last time!'

'Please!' whispered Greta. 'We need you! I need you! Grandma needs you!'

'It's the only way,' I said, pointing to Greta's mother.

'WHEEEEE-HEEEE!' Greta's mother squealed, as she somersaulted upside down.

'Gaaa! Fine!' grumbled Grandpa Woebegone,

walking over to me. 'But you best let me out this time!'

He jabbed a finger at me and then stepped *inside* me. Percy sighed, then followed suit, melding his spirit with mine.

I immediately felt my energy increase and the air started to crackle.

I let the power flow through me and I could not help but let out a cackle of delight.

I threw my hands in the air, and this time the pictures came flying off the wall.

Books flew into the air and teacups smashed against the windows.

Pussy Lanimous jumped off Greta's father's lap with a yowl and raced for the door, but I slammed it shut before the cat could escape. It spun round, trying to find a new way out.

But there was no escape.

With a flick of my wrist I levitated the cat two metres into the air – a whirling, howling, spinning ball of fur and claws.

Then the table started hovering, and the sofa smashed against the mantelpiece.

Greta's mother was screaming as she finally realized it was not her chakras making her float, but something far more sinister.

ME!

I could taste her fear and it was delectable.

Larry floated into the air too, but he did not seem bothered, because he was chasing a lorry that was also floating near him.

Greta's father wheeled out from under his desk, panic etched on his face.

'Help meeee!' screamed Greta's mother. 'Get me downnnnnn!'

The room was a tornado of cats and books and pictures and mothers and cups and saucers and brothers. A stray poo-covered stick managed to whack Greta's mother on the face. I could not resist giving her nose a hard pinch and she yelped in pain. The noise was tremendous as tables smashed against walls, and crockery hit windows.

Greta's father had grabbed his wife's foot and was trying to pull her down. With a final blast of energy coursing through me I directed it at Greta's father. As he felt his wheelchair leave the floor, he let go of his wife and gripped on to the arms, and began spinning and gyrating through the air. As he twisted upside down, I could see he was clinging on for dear life, screaming through gritted teeth. Pussy Lanimous was back in his lap somehow, claws dug into his legs, meowing with terror.

What I am trying to say is that it was all utterly hilarious.

Sadly, though, I was beginning to tire, so as suddenly as I had started it, I stopped. Everything flying around the room came crashing down in one smashing, howling and meowing heap.

Greta's mother sat up, panting in fear, black mascara streaking down her cheeks.

'Th-this p-place,' she stammered, wiping her pale face. 'This place is h-h-haunted!'

Finally!

Greta turned and gave me two thumbs up.

Pussy Lanimous bolted out of the room, closely followed by Greta's mother and father.

Greta jumped in the air. 'It worked!'

I smiled to myself. My reign as the most terrifying ghost in the house continued unchallenged. I flexed my fingers, enjoying the power the other spirits gave me.

Greta eyed me suspiciously. 'Wolfgang, it's time to let the others out,' she said.

'*Nein,*' I said. 'I think not.' I did not want to give up this feeling.

'Wolfgang,' Greta said sternly, 'let them go. Or I will make a special lorry track in the cellar for Larry, so he's ALWAYS there with you.'

'Gah! Fine,' I conceded.

I unlocked the corner of my spirit where Grandpa Woebegone and Percy were trapped, and they both immediately sprang out of me.

'Yech!' said Grandpa Woebegone, dusting himself down. 'That was dreadful.'

Percy shuddered. 'I need a bath.'

So rude.

CHAPTER
12

Greta's mother called a family meeting the next morning after breakfast.

She sipped at her tea, her hands still trembling, the cup rattling on the saucer. Greta's father looked serious, his face – behind the beard – pale and drawn. Larry looked unconcerned – he was playing with a car today, presumably in an attempt to add a little variety to his monotonous life. Greta sat waiting impatiently.

'Thank you all for coming to this family meeting,' Greta's mother said unnecessarily. 'I'm afraid –'

'Mother,' interrupted Greta. 'How come when you call a family meeting, you never include Grandma?

She's just upstairs, you know, and just as much a part of this family as any of us!'

'Yes, dear, but it's . . . it's too difficult to get her downstairs.'

'But we could just have the meeting up–'

'Now don't interrupt dear,' snapped her mother with a fly-swatting edge to her voice. 'I have something to tell you all,' she continued, closing her eyes and holding one hand up dramatically. 'This . . . this house is . . . haunted!'

'I know! I have been trying to tell you that for *ages*,' said Greta.

'Don't answer back to your mother,' Greta's father said.

'I wasn't answering back!'

'Don't answer back to your father,' Greta's mother said.

'I wasn't answering back!!'

'Lorries!' shouted Larry.

'Not lorries, poppet,' wailed Greta's mother. 'Ghosts!'

'I told you so,' said Greta. 'I told you Grandma and

I could see them. Well, now you can see Grandma *isn't* losing her marbles. And that means you can't send her off to some nursing home. That means she has to stay! Isn't that right, Father?'

'Well . . . I . . . errr . . . I, er . . . I suppose so . . .' he stammered.

Greta's mother groaned. 'Noooo . . . My beautiful new yoga studio . . .'

Greta jumped up and whooped. 'YESSSSS! I'm going to go and tell her!'

She bounded up the steps two at a time until she arrived at Grandma Woebegone's bedroom. She burst in and blurted out how her plan had succeeded.

'Well, that is just the most wonderful news!' cried Grandma. 'I shall unpack my things. I'm so relieved. I don't have to leave my home. Or Grandpa. Isn't that right, darling?'

'Erm . . . he's not in the room, Grandma,' said Greta.

'Yes, I knew that,' said Grandma, who did not know that.

'Well, I shall leave you to unpack,' said Greta

happily. 'But I'm so pleased you're not going anywhere.'

She skipped back down to the kitchen, where her parents were talking as her mother scrolled on her phone.

'I can't believe there are ghosts in this house,' Greta's mother groaned. 'It's like when Greta got nits.'

'Or when Pussy Lanimous got fleas,' added Greta's father.

'They are not like nits and fleas! They're people!' protested Greta. 'Well, ghost people.'

'No, Greta,' her father said. 'They are unwanted visitors.'

'Exactly!' her mother agreed. 'And I'm going to get rid of them if it's the last thing I do!'

She stabbed at her phone and raised it to her ear. 'Hello? Yes, I hope you *can* help me. I have an infestation at my home. Yes, they *are* vermin! And I need your help to exterminate them.' She paused while she listened, and then she continued. 'And you can guarantee to rid

any house of ghosts? Oh, that's marvellous. Yes, come as quick as you can!'

She put down the phone and gave a smile lacking any hint of warmth. 'There, that should do it!'

And then it finally hit Greta. Like a penny dropped from the very top of the Eiffel Tower. She gasped and ran all the way back upstairs again.

'Grandma!' she wailed as she burst into the

attic. 'What have I done? It wasn't good news at all! They've called an exterminator! To get rid of the ghosts! And that means they'll get rid of Grandpa Woebegone too!' Greta looked like she was about to burst into tears.

Grandma Woebegone took her hand. 'There, there. But Grandpa has been waiting for such a long time – maybe it's his time to pass over to the other side?'

'But, Grandma, you'd be lonely without him,' Greta said, holding her grandmother's hand to her face. It felt so fragile: sparrow-boned, the skin loose and papery.

'Greta, loss is part of life. It's the natural way of things. And anyway, I'll be with him soon.'

'No! Don't say that, Grandma!'

Grandma smiled gently. 'Time is the one thing you can't argue with, my dear. And I've had plenty enough of it.'

Greta spent much of the morning in her room, railing at the shortness of life, blubbing and sobbing.

And it's true: life can be hard sometimes. Sadness hides round corners ready to pounce when you least expect it. But I mean have you *ever* known a child to cry quite so *much* as her?

It was time, I thought, to really give her something to cry about.

'Child . . .' I whispered in her ear. 'Hear me . . .'

Greta wiped her eyes. 'I've told you to stop that whispering nonsense. It's very silly.'

'What*ever*,' I said. I had learned to say that recently, and I thought it made me sound deliciously wicked.

'You sound like a moody teenager,' Greta said.

'What*everrr*,' I repeated. 'Talk to the hand.' Another deliciously wicked phrase I had picked up. 'Anyway, I suggest you listen very carefully to what I have to say.'

'What is it then?' she asked.

'What your parents are planning is something called an exorcism. An exorcism is the word for when you forcefully get rid of ghosts.'

'OK,' Greta said. 'And?'

'Well, child, if a ghost is exorcized, they don't pass over to the other side. They simply blink out of existence,' I said with a click of my fingers. Unfortunately because I was a ghost it made no noise, so it lost some of its impact. 'Completely. Forever.'

Greta looked at me and swallowed. She was beginning to understand.

'And that means that when your grandmother dies, Grandpa will not be there waiting for her on the other side. For them, there will be no happy ending.'

CHAPTER
13

When I informed Grandpa of this latest news, he was not best pleased.

'I said this would happen! Didn't I say no good would come from all this haunting? You said it would be fine, didn't you? Well, it's *not* fine, is it? In fact, it's very far from fine. That's what happens when you take risks, see?'

I was in no mood to hang around such a Moaning Marlene, so I decided to see if Greta was any cheerier.

Now, after receiving this devastating news, you *might* imagine that Greta would spend the rest of the day moping about miserably.

And you would be absolutely right.

It started with sobbing into a pillow, and slowly

progressed to staring out of the window of the sitting room, looking mournfully at some children playing in the street.

'Why don't you go and join them?' asked her mother. 'Get some sun on your skin. You're getting paler by the day. You look like you're about to disappear.'

'I told you,' Greta replied sullenly. 'I'm not ready yet.'

'Fine,' her mother said, walking out of the room. 'Suit yourself.'

Grandpa Woebegone, who had been sitting in the armchair, gave Greta a long, old-person's questioning stare – the sort of look that was meant to show seriousness and wisdom and caring, but really just made him look like he was trying to remember if he'd turned the oven off before he'd left the house.

'What?' growled Greta. 'I'm not well enough yet, OK?'

Grandpa Woebegone held his hands up as if he weren't doing anything.

Eventually, though, Greta got back her annoyingly plucky and determined spirit.

She found me in my cellar, playing with little Ludwig. She rolled up the sleeves of her dress, marched straight over to me and said, with impressive steeliness in her voice and a very serious look in her eyes, 'Well, I'm not going to let that exorcist stuff happen. And nor,' she continued, mixing things up by having a steely look in her eyes and a very serious voice, 'are *you.*'

Ordinarily I would not allow myself to be bossed around by an uppity child, but it did appear that for now our causes were aligned. She did not want her grandpa to be exorcized into nothingness. I did not want me to be exorcized into nothingness.

Nobody cared about Percy.

'I care about Percy!' argued Greta when I pointed this out to her later in a meeting with her and Grandpa Woebegone.

'Why? He's an insignificant child covered in ugly boils –'

'FORSOOTH, I'M SITTING RIGHT HERE,' said Percy.

'You see!' I said, throwing my hands in the air. 'I didn't even notice him! This proves my point. Totally insignificant.'

An ingenious plan suddenly jumped fully formed into my brilliant mind. 'You know, we could allow *Percy* to be exorcized. You know, sacrifice him, so that we are left alone? Everyone is happy!'

'*I* wouldn't be!' protested Percy.

'So?' I said, slightly baffled. 'You know,' I whispered to Greta, 'are you sure about keeping the old man?' I nodded in Grandpa Woebegone's direction. 'He smells a bit weird.'

'We will NOT be allowing Percy or Grandpa – or *any* ghost for that matter – to be exorcized from this house,' Greta said, glaring at me. 'We all stick *together*. Agreed, everyone?'

Quiet sliced through the room like a guillotine. Percy and Grandpa glowered at me.

Eventually Percy said sullenly, 'Agreed.'

Grandpa threw daggers at me but then said through gritted teeth, 'Fine. Agreed.'

I should point out he did not *literally* throw daggers. It is a phrase that means he scowled at me. And anyway, as you know, he is a *common* ghost not a poltergeist, so can't even pick up daggers, never mind throw them.

But I digress . . .

So all the attention was on me.

'Well?' Greta said, drumming her fingers. Even though I am a two-hundred-year-old ghost, there was something intimidating about her. The balance of power was all wrong.

'OK! Yes! Whatever. We stick together,' I said.

We did not realize, though, how quickly our little team was going to be tested.

Later that very same day, there was a ring at the doorbell.

Greta was lying on the sofa reading a book. Her father was tapping away at the typewriter. Her brother had built a ramp out of books and was driving a lorry up and down it.

'Ooh!' exclaimed Greta's mother, springing up from her chair like a flea in a frying pan. 'She's here!' She practically ran to the door.

'Who's here?' Greta asked her father.

'Somebody who can sort out this ghost problem. An exorcist, I believe she's called.'

'What? No! If they exorcize the ghosts, she'll kill them!'

'She can't kill them if they're already dead,' snapped her father.

'But –'

Before Greta could finish her sentence, her

mother wafted back into the room, followed by a woman half her size. The woman was tiny – no taller than Greta – and round, with thick glasses and a beehive hairdo. She was carrying a small, depressed-looking bunch of flowers, which looked themselves to be in need of exorcism, and had a huge rucksack on her back that gave her the appearance of a short-sighted beetle.

'This is –' Greta's mother began, before she was interrupted by the stranger's loud, squeaky voice.

'My name is Magda Carter. I am a medium.'

'You look more like an extra-small to me,' Greta's father said, eyeing her.

'I don't mean medium size! I mean, I am a medium that can speak to spirits. And I am here to rid your home of all unwelcome ghosts.'

She proceeded to shake the flowers at each corner of the room. Then she began sniffing – everything. And each time she sniffed, she would mutter to herself.

'Ah yes . . .' she murmured, sniffing the sofa.

'Hmmm . . .' she said, sniffing the bookcase.

172

'Maybe . . .'

'Oh, goodness gracious me, no, no, no,' she muttered, sniffing Greta.

'Yuck,' she said after sniffing Pussy Lanimous. 'Your cat smells dreadful.'

The cat gave her a death stare and scrambled under the sofa.

Without warning Magda Carter turned and strutted out into the hall, leaving Greta open-mouthed. After a moment, the family all quickly hurried after her, as she went from room to room all around the house, sniffing and flower-quivering.

Eventually they arrived back at the sitting room, where Magda Carter instructed the overawed (Greta's mother and father) and baffled (Greta and Larry) family to sit.

They did as they were told.

Magda Carter took a deep breath and closed her eyes before she spoke.

'This house has many hearts,' she announced.

'Oh, that's nice,' said Greta's father. 'Do you

hear that, Prosecca? She said the –'

'Silence!' squeaked Magda Carter, opening her eyes and glaring at Greta's father. 'You must not interrupt.'

By now Percy and Grandpa Woebegone had joined us, no doubt to see what this stranger had to say for herself, and whether she was the one who would bring a final death to us ghosts.

The moment they entered, Magda Carter started sniffing more quickly, like a hound that had caught the scent of a fox. Percy and Grandpa edged away from her nervously.

'The first thing that you need to know,' continued Magda Carter, still sniffing, 'is there is no such thing as death.'

'No death?' said Grandpa. 'What a load of old rot. I couldn't be more dead if I tried!'

I had to agree with the terrible-smelling old man. I was also very dead.

Magda Carter continued, closing her eyes again. 'There is only a transition to a different sphere of consciousness.'

'What *is* she banging on about?' asked Grandpa. 'A different sphere of *what*?'

Magda Carter gave a little shudder. 'These poor souls who are not at rest linger in a perpetual dream, a nightmare from which they cannot awake.'

'A nightmare?' said Percy. ''Tis not *that* bad.'

'I don't know – with your boiley face and the smell of Grandpa Woebegone, it feels pretty nightmarish to me,' I said.

'Shush!' snapped Greta. 'Don't be so mean.'

Magda Carter's owlish eyes swung round and focused on Greta.

'You! Who were you talking to?'

'Nobody,' said Greta nervously.

'Your mother tells me you have been conversing with the spirits,' said Magda, eyeing Greta through her thick glasses.

'Yes, I –'

'Well, don't. You'll only end up getting yourself possessed and then I will have to charge your parents double for spirit removal.'

'Greta,' said her mother urgently. 'You must never

talk to another ghost again!'

'One more thing,' Magda said, holding up a tiny plump finger, 'I sense more than one ghost. There is a terrible presence in this house. Foul and evil . . .'

'Grandpa, I think she is talking about your weird smell,' I said fairly.

Grandpa Woebegone made a rather ungentlemanly hand gesture towards me, which I thought reflected very poorly on him.

'She's talking about you, you nincompoop!' he whispered at me.

Nein! Surely not! And how dare he call me a nincompoop?!

'A wicked creature,' Magda continued, 'with a black, rotten heart . . .'

Ah. Perhaps she *was* talking about me.

'. . . full of misery and despair. A being without hope . . .'

Ja. She was *definitely* talking about me. The description was uncanny.

Greta gave me a knowing look and a nod as if to say, *Yes, you have been rather nincompoopish, Wolfgang.*

'But I shall guide that creature, and the rest of the spirits, through a window to the next plane.'

Percy gasped. 'No! I'll not have this witch put us on a devil's flying machine!'

'I don't think she means an aeroplane,' Greta said to Percy gently.

'Of course I don't mean an aeroplane, silly child!' snapped Magda Carter. 'I mean, I shall help them pass over to the other side, from the earthbound to the spirit world! And my one-hundred-per-cent-guaranteed-or-your-money-back ceremony will begin immediately!'

CHAPTER 14

Rain drummed hard on the windows, as Magda Carter lit candles and dimmed the lights.

'That'll be to calm the spirits,' Greta's mother said, nodding knowledgeably.

Magda Carter lit incense, which coiled its way through the house like a snake.

'That'll be to cleanse the aura of the building,' Greta's mother said, nodding knowledgeably.

Magda Carter dragged a table into the centre of the sitting room.

'That'll be for a relaxing game of ping-pong before she begins,' Greta's mother said, nodding unknowledgeably. 'Or maybe tiddlywinks.'

'No, Mrs Woebegone, there will be no time for

games,' corrected Magda Carter. 'This table is where I shall communicate with the ghosts!'

She threw a tablecloth over the table, placed a candle in the centre and dimmed the lights even more.

'Now,' she said, turning to the Woebegone family, 'I want you all to bring me something important to you, something you treasure.'

Greta's father wheeled over and dropped his pipe on his table.

To Greta's wide-eyed surprise, her mother lifted a framed photo of Greta and Larry from the dresser. She gazed at it for a moment, then plonked it back down and picked up the box that it had sat on – her most precious crystals – which she carefully placed on the table as gently as if it were a newborn baby.

Larry dropped a lorry beside it.

Greta thought for a moment, then bounded up the stairs. She didn't want to bring anything too important to her, in case it actually helped the medium, but they all had to *think* it was.

Greta knew exactly the right thing – she stretched up to the top of her wardrobe and grabbed her Whoopsie-Daisy doll with its staring eyes and long arms.

Returning to the sitting room, she put the doll in the centre of the table, away from the flickering flame of the candle.

Magda Carter told everybody to sit down at the table and place their hands flat on the surface, which they all dutifully did, except Larry, who was quickly packed off to bed.

The candle in the centre of the table created huge trembling shadows on the walls and bookcases. Greta shivered. I could feel her nerves. Worry and care were etched in her face.

What happens if this odd little woman actually can rid the house of all the spirits? she thought. *Will it be the end of Grandpa, Percy and Wolfgang?*

Well, dear child, we shall have to see about that.

'Quiet!' barked Magda Carter, even though the only sound was the wind howling outside. 'I need absolute silence from now on. The slightest noise could break the seance!'

Greta gave a large, fake-sounding sneeze.

Magda Carter glared at her.

'Sorry,' Greta whispered. Even Percy could see she didn't mean it.

'Whatever happens, do not leave this table,' warned the medium, 'or a spirit may leap into your body, with untold financial implications. I may go into a slight trance. That's perfectly normal – do NOT interrupt me. Now let us begin!' She paused for effect. She was quite the actor, I will give her that. 'Is there anybody out there? Spirits, come to me! Give one knock for yes, two for no!'

Ha! What ghost would be so foolish as to give themselves away by doing that?

Percy.

Percy would.

He knocked hard once on the table.

Greta's mother let out a little scream, and her father nearly fell out of his wheelchair.

'Good grief,' he said, his face pale as candle

wax. 'I don't believe it!'

I sent a look of fury at Percy.

'Alas, I couldn't help it!' he pleaded. 'She made me do it!'

'Well, don't do it again!' I warned.

A flash of lightning framed the curtains, followed by a low rumble of thunder.

'And how many spirits are in this house?' continued the medium. 'Knock, spirit, I command you!'

Percy gave three sharp knocks on the table.

He grabbed his hand and pulled it away. 'She made me again!' he wailed, pointing at the medium.

Greta's mother gave a little whimper of terror.

'Three spirits roam this house!' roared Magda Carter. 'And in thunder, lightning and rain, three spirits shall be banished on this night!'

She pulled a needle from her pocket and stabbed it into her finger. 'By the pricking of my thumb, rid this house of ghostly scum!'

A terrible sensation suddenly flooded my body,

as if something had taken a bite out of my soul. I heard gasps from Percy and Grandpa Woebegone – clearly they had felt the same dreadful feeling.

It could only mean one thing – this woman actually knew what she was doing. She was going to exorcize us!

Greta saw the fear in all our faces. 'No!' she cried, jumping up.

'SIT DOWN!' ordered Magda Carter.

'Do what she says!' snapped Greta's mother.

Greta reluctantly sat down again and slowly

placed her hands back on the table.

'We must do something!' wailed Percy, as a clap of thunder rattled the windows.

'But what?' asked Grandpa Woebegone.

A smile crept on to my devilishly handsome face. 'I know . . .'

If there was one thing I could do, it was drive people out of this house. There was, of course, Great-aunt Irma Woebegone, a sweet joyful woman that I took great pleasure in tormenting, until she ran sobbing from here, her mind twisted with fear, her heart pounding with terror, her knickers soiled with poo.

Happy days. I sighed at the memory.

So, I must terrify this Magda Carter.

I first pushed Larry's lorry across the table slowly, slowly – just for show.

Greta's mother moaned with fear.

Then, one by one, I blew in each of their ears, sending shivers through them.

I paused behind the medium and tried stepping

inside her mind, and she immediately
fell into a trance.

She was strong – I could feel her
spirit battling against me.

It was too strong for me. She threw
me out and I lay panting on the floor.

I summoned up more strength and
threw ectoplasm at her and everybody
round the table.

'What is *this*?' screeched Greta's
mother, wiping slime off her face.

'It's ectoplasm,' said Greta matter-of-factly.

'It looks like you've sneezed all over them,'
Percy said.

And to be fair it did indeed look
like they had been sneezed upon. By
an elephant.

'Begone, foul demons!' Magda
Carter cried.

'Here, who are you calling "foul"?' asked
Grandpa Woebegone. 'The cheek of it!'

'Begone, accursed spirits haunting this pure, sweet family!' Magda Carter cried again.

Pure, sweet family? Had she *met* them?

She smashed her fists on the table and it felt like a gunshot wound to our souls. I saw Grandpa Woebegone stagger.

Do something! mouthed Greta desperately.

And that is when I knew.

I had to use the single creepiest, most terrifying thing imaginable – Greta's Whoopsie-Daisy doll.

I closed my eyes and concentrated.

The doll stood up on the table, wobbling slightly.

Its eyes winked: first one, then the other.

And then it walked, a grin painted on its porcelain face, its arms outstretched towards Magda Carter.

She tried to back her chair away in terror, but the doll jumped across the table, landed in her lap and seized her in a bear hug.

Magda jumped up and tried to pull the doll off her, but I was not letting go that easily.

Greta's father wheeled round and grabbed hold of the legs of the doll. With one gigantic tug he managed to pull it free, and sent it sailing across the room and into a heap in the corner.

'Whoopsie-daisy!' the doll said, and then proceeded to do a wee on the carpet – which was nothing to do with me but merely a design feature.

Magda Carter staggered to her feet, panting. She stared in terror at the doll, now lying still on the floor.

Then the doll twitched, and slowly began crawling towards Magda, who let out a blood-curdling scream.

She grabbed her backpack and turned to Greta's parents. 'Sorry,' she said. 'You're on your own!'

And without a look back, Magda Carter fled Woebegone Hall into the howling rain, never to be seen again.

'Well,' said Greta's father, picking up his pipe, 'looks like we'll be getting our money back after all.'

CHAPTER
15

But Greta's parents were not about to give up that easily. The sound of Magda Carter slamming the door was still ringing in our ears when her mother started prowling around the room, jabbing her finger at where she thought we ghosts might be standing.

'You think you've won? Well, let me tell you, you haven't! I am not going to lose this war! This is *my* house and you are *leaving* whether you like it or *not*, or my name isn't Prosecca Woebegone!'

She stormed out of the room, leaving the rest of us in silence.

I almost felt bad for her, but of course I actually didn't.

She was clearly a determined, strong woman, and these are qualities I always admire in a person. Apart from when that person is Greta Woebegone, and then I just find them annoying.

'We have to keep going,' Greta said determinedly and strongly. 'And whatever my parents throw at us, we stick together and fight as one!'

You see? *Such* a goody two shoes.

Next morning, I was in my cellar, chatting to little Ludwig, who was nibbling on a small lump of something nameless, his tiny whiskers twitching and quivering.

I may be an evil spirit who has haunted countless generations over centuries, but his adorable furry face melts my heart. I bent down until I was nearly nose to nose with him.

'That's right, sweet little Ludwig. Are you happy today, *mein Liebling*?'

'Yes, thank you,' he squeaked. 'Apart from being stuck in a cellar with a mildly depressed German ghost who won't leave me alone for two seconds.'

'You are so funny, little Ludwig! Now you want Daddy Wolfgang to find you some cheese? Daddy Wolfgang get some cheese for pretty little Lud– WHAT ARE YOU ALL DOING IN HERE?!'

Percy, Grandpa Woebegone and Greta were standing at the bottom of the stairs staring at me.

'AND WHY ARE YOU ALL STARING AT ME LIKE THAT?'

Grandpa Woebegone was sniggering, and Greta could only be described as beaming from ear to ear.

'Oh, Wolfgang, I knew it! You do have a heart!' she said, and right at that moment I had never hated anyone more than I hated her.

'WHAT ARE YOU DOING SNEAKING INTO MY CELLAR, SPYING ON ME?'

'We're not spying on you,' said Greta. 'We were just coming down to have a team meeting.'

'A bit of a debrief, post-seance,' said Grandpa Woebegone. 'Just you, me, Greta, Percy and sweet little Ludwig!' He roared with laughter.

Correction: right at that moment I had never hated anyone more than I hated Grandpa Woebegone. I

could see even Percy sniggering behind his hand.

I glared at him and he soon stopped.

Ludwig scuttered over and jumped on Percy, who yelped, but then started stroking Ludwig, who looked very content and happy for a treacherous rodent.

'I'm surprised you are so relaxed with stroking that rat.' Greta laughed.

'Why? 'Tis rather sweet,' Percy replied.

'Well, you know . . . what with you dying of the plague, and rats being to blame for the Black Death.'

'WHAT DID YOU SAY?' Percy yelled.

'Well, it wasn't the rats themselves, but the fleas on the rats that spread the plague, and –'

'YECCCCHHHHHH!' Percy jumped up and flung poor, sweet little Ludwig away from him across the room.

Fortunately for the treacherous little rat, he landed right in my lap. He ran into my pocket and we continued the meeting, with Percy glaring at me throughout.

Despite our relief at sending Magda Carter packing, there was worry about what Prosecca's threat about 'not losing the war' might mean.

Well, I wasn't worried, but Grandpa Woebegone was.

'There's trouble ahead,' he warned.

Good.

Let them bring trouble.

I sent them out of my cellar so I could have some privacy and hatch some dark plans for revenge for all their roaring and sniggering.

Percy went off to do goodness knows what – probably play that dreadful game where he pushes poo around with a stick.

Later, I found Grandpa Woebegone and Greta sitting with her grandma. I had slipped through the house like smoke, seeped slowly through the keyhole of Grandma's room, and settled on the ceiling, where I could not be seen.

Greta and Grandma Woebegone were playing poker.

Grandpa Woebegone was standing behind

Grandma and peeking at her cards.

'Careful, Greta! She has a pair of queens!'

'Stop telling me what she's got, Grandpa,' admonished Greta.

Grandma gave a little giggle. 'He was terrible at cards,' she whispered. 'Always trying to cheat.'

'How dare you!' shouted Grandpa. 'I've never cheated in my life!'

Greta grinned. She didn't believe him and nor did I.

'Grandma,' said Greta, the grin falling from her face, 'there's something I need to tell you. If Mother and Father succeed in getting rid of the ghosts, well, Grandpa will be gone.'

'Yes. Gone to the other side.'

'No. That's just it. If ghosts are exorcized, they vanish *completely*. They don't pass over to the other side.'

Grandma went pale. 'So he won't be there when I . . .'

Greta shook her head. 'He'll be gone forever,' she said. 'That's why we are going to stop them!'

Grandma nodded solemnly and gave her a watery thank-you smile. 'Poor Grandpa,' she said. 'He doesn't deserve an end like that – just disappearing. He led such a hard life.'

'Nonsense!' shouted Grandpa.

'But he never liked to talk about it,' said Grandma.

'Balderdash!' hollered Grandpa.

'Would you tell me about him, Grandma?' asked Greta. 'It might help.'

Grandma paused for a moment, lost in thought. 'It was a life peppered with tragedy, really,' she began. 'Grandpa lost both his parents at a young age. Your great-grandpa smoked like a chimney and died when Grandpa was only seven. Your great-grandmother died when your grandpa was ten – in a train crash, of all things. Imagine – your poor grandfather, orphaned by the age of ten.'

'Come on!' harrumphed Grandpa Woebegone. 'Get on with the game! We don't have time for all this chit-chat.'

'He also had a brother,' continued Grandma.

'They were very close. But he lost him in the war. He'd lost everybody.'

'Can we *please* talk about something else? I really don't want to have to listen to all this . . . ancient history!' moaned Grandpa.

'Well, losing his whole family like that, it's not surprising he was so anxious. So careful. So afraid. It's not surprising he wanted me to give up racing, I suppose.'

'CAN WE STOP THIS?' Grandpa bellowed,

standing up abruptly. 'I . . . I . . . did what I had to do!' he barked and stormed out of the room.

Grandma sighed, and looked out of the window. 'He was so full of love, but the more he loved something, the more terrified he was of losing it. We even had a dog – a beautiful beagle called Misty – and he doted on that little mutt, but he never let her off the leash once. Not even at the beach. Misty was such a good dog,' Grandma added, her eyes glistening with tears.

Before Greta could say anything, her mother bellowed from downstairs.

'Greta Woebegone! Come down here at once!'

'Sorry, Grandma. I have to go. But Misty sounds like a very good dog indeed,' Greta said, and then trudged obediently down the stairs, finding her parents in the kitchen.

'Just to let you know, we have more . . . *visitors* this evening,' her mother said.

'Who?' asked Greta in a quiet voice.

'Well, after that useless Carter woman,' said Greta's father, sucking on his unlit pipe, 'I thought it was time to bring in some real experts. You know – people who will get the job done. *Professionals.*'

'And,' said her mother, wagging her finger at Greta, 'we don't want you trying to spoil it this time.'

'What? I never –'

'Don't try to pretend with me, young lady. I saw you with your little coughs and fake sneezes. I'll be keeping a very close eye on you, and if I spot you doing *anything* to help your little ghost friends, you'll be in more trouble than you can possibly imagine.'

Greta spent the rest of the afternoon wondering and worrying about who would be coming to the house. The minutes trickled by, slowly turning into hours, until dusk was squeezing the last breath out of the day and, finally, the sound of a van pulling up outside caused Greta's heart to start thumping.

She ran to the window and peered through the smudgy grime.

'Are they here?' asked Percy nervously.

Parked outside was a silver van, emblazoned

down the side with the words SPIRIT SMASHERS in big black letters. Underneath were smaller letters that said SPIRIT-KICKIN' GOOD.

The doors of the van opened and two men stepped out. They were dressed completely in black, with black coats and black hats. The wind blew leaves around their feet, while clouds above them darkened in the dying embers of the day. The taller of the two slid open the side door of the van and grabbed a large plain black bag.

They stood next to each other on the pavement and, as one, looked the house up and down. The smaller of the two caught sight of Greta, who ducked down underneath the windowsill.

A moment later, the doorbell rang.

Greta turned and nodded to Percy, not able to hide the fear in her eyes.

Whoever they were, they were here.

'Greta, darling? Would you mind coming down?'

It was Greta's mother, calling her from the bottom of the stairs.

Greta closed her eyes. She did not want to go

downstairs, and she did not want to meet these two strangers.

'Greta! Darling! Come downstairs now! Please!'

The way her mother said 'please!' indicated it was not, in fact, a request and was, in fact, an order, so Greta knew she had no choice. It was time to meet the Spirit Smashers.

As she walked into the sitting room, Percy and Grandpa Woebegone were already there, standing nervously in the corner. I slid in behind Greta like a shadow.

Greta's parents gave her a quick smile. The Spirit Smashers gave her a beady stare. Basically everybody was looking at Greta.

'Hello,' said Greta nervously.

'Now is not the time for hellos!' thundered the shorter Spirit Smasher. 'Not when evil walks the rooms of this house!'

'Steady on!' said Grandpa Woebegone.

'My name,' said the shorter Spirit Smasher, who had slicked-back black hair that glistened in the soft light of the room, 'is Professor Max Sydown.

But you may call me Professor Sydown.'

'And my name is Chris,' said the taller Spirit Smasher. 'But you may call me –' he stopped for a second, his eyes narrowing thoughtfully – 'Chris.'

'You have called us here to solve your paranormal predicament,' said Professor Sydown. 'Well, you came to the right people. We are the Spirit Smashers and we smash spirits and chew gum. And I'm all out of gum.'

'No, you're not,' said Chris.

'What?' asked Professor Sydown.

'You're not out of gum. You've got some in your back pocket. I saw you put it there before getting out of the van.'

'It's just a phrase! I didn't actually mean I was out of gum.'

'Ah,' said Chris. 'Understood.'

This was a lie. His soft blue eyes, sitting under a mop of blond hair, had all the understanding of a turkey waiting for the Boxing Day sales.

'You!' said Professor Sydown, pointing at Greta. 'I am told you have been helping the evil spirits.'

'They aren't evil; they are my friends,' said Greta. 'And if you get rid of them, they will be gone forever!'

'My dear child,' said Professor Sydown, approaching Greta and putting a not-friendly hand on her shoulder, 'of course we will get rid of them. That's our job. And we're here not a moment too soon, as they have clearly got into your head. Now, Chris, please pass me the bag.'

Chris walked over and passed it to him.

Professor Sydown opened the bag and pulled from it what appeared to be a large dead fish.

'Chris. There appears to be a large dead fish

in our Spirit Smashers equipment bag.'

'Oh, I wondered where that had got to,' said Chris.

'Chris, why is there a large dead fish in our Spirit Smashers bag?'

'I must have accidentally put it in there after my volunteering at the zoo. I was feeding the penguins.'

Professor Sydown glared at Chris, and then pulled out a bunch of bananas. 'For the monkeys?' asked Professor Sydown, glaring even harder.

Chris nodded.

'And . . . this?' Professor Sydown said, holding up a nappy. He gave it a sniff and pulled a face.

'That's from the baby monkey,' said Chris. 'He's very cute.'

'Chris, would it be fair to say you have managed to get our Spirit Smashers equipment bag mixed up with your zoo bag?'

'That's very possible, Professor Sydown,' said Chris, looking nervous.

'I've told you before, Chris,' Professor Sydown

said, waggling a stumpy finger, 'if your volunteering at the zoo starts to negatively impact your work, we are going to have to make you choose between being a zookeeper and a Spirit Smasher.'

Chris looked ashen. 'No!'

'Yes! And now look – we haven't got our equipment!'

'This is most disappointing,' said Greta's mother to her husband. 'You said that these people were professionals. This isn't a particularly professional start.'

'I assure you, Mr and Mrs Woebegone,' said Professor Sydown, bowing his head slightly, 'we are professionals of the *highest* order. We don't usually mess up quite so spectacularly.'

'I don't know about that,' said Chris. 'Remember when we accidentally untied the Possessed Goat of Blinkington Hall, and it knocked Sir Humphrey Blinkington out of the window and straight into the fertilizer pit?'

'Well, now's not the time to –'

'And what about when we accidentally unleashed

that demon in the town hall on the day of the Women's Institute Christmas raffle? Those grannies never recovered.'

'Yes, but –'

'And then there was that time in the cathedral when you got possessed by a spirit and pulled a moonie at the Archbishop of York, and then did a wee in the font –'

'CHRISTOPHER! I am sure the Woebegones do NOT want to hear all these stories!'

'Actually I wouldn't mind,' said Greta, grinning widely. 'They sound *fascinating*.'

'Well, I'm afraid we don't have time to dilly-dally around, sharing old gossip,' Professor Sydown said, glaring at Chris. 'Because thanks to a certain careless Spirit Smasher, we now have to go back to the zoo to find and rescue the Spirit Smashers equipment bag.'

'Thinking about it, there's a small chance I might have left it in the orangutan enclosure.'

'A *small* chance?'

'Actually, thinking about it, a big chance. A very

big chance. In fact, I am almost certainly, definitely sure I left it in the orangutan enclosure.'

'Great. Marvellous. We now have to rescue the Spirit Smashers equipment bag from the orangutan enclosure!'

Professor Sydown stormed out, muttering to himself furiously about orangutans, closely followed by a shame-faced Chris.

An hour later, the van pulled up again and after a moment the doorbell rang.

In walked Chris with a huge rip in his black suit, which was now covered in orange fur, followed by Professor Sydown, who was sporting a recently blackened eye, and whose previously perfect hair was now like a bird's nest in a storm.

'Things go well in the orangutan enclosure?' asked Greta, grinning again.

'No, young *lady*, they did not. At. All.' Professor Sydown glowered at Greta. 'But, no matter – we are back now. And we shall now begin the banishing of the spirits from this house. First, a quick prayer.

Chris, would you mind passing me the Bible?'

'The Bible?'

'Yes, Chris. The Bible. Quickly!'

'Er . . . You mean the Bible you were using to hit the orangutan with when you were getting attacked?'

'Yes. That one.'

'You left it in the orangutan enclosure.'

Another hour later, the van pulled up once again, and in walked Chris and Professor Sydown, holding a soggy-looking Bible that looked very much like it had been chewed by a hungry orangutan.

'Right!' said Professor Sydown, holding up a finger. 'This time we *definitely* have everything! Now, first we have to rid this child of her demonic presence.'

'EXCUSE ME?!' exclaimed Greta.

'Ever since I first set foot in this house,' Professor Sydown said, pointing at Greta, 'I have felt an evil atmosphere coming from this child.'

'I knew it! I told you there was something odd about her,' said Greta's mother, nudging her husband.

He nodded, chewing thoughtfully on his pipe.

'Mother!' said Greta.

'But a quick blast with this should sort you out in a jiffy,' said Professor Sydown, rummaging in the equipment bag and pulling out what looked like a huge gun with electronic lights.

Greta gasped. 'What's that?'

'It's nothing to worry about.' Professor Sydown laughed good-naturedly. 'It's just a simple laser-guided evil-targeting spirit blaster that uses high-level radioactive microwave beams. I invented it. And it's very safe. Almost definitely.'

'You are not shooting that thing at me!' protested Greta. 'And anyway, there is absolutely nothing wrong with me!' she said, folding her arms.

'Don't argue with the nice Spirit Smasher, dear,' said Greta's mother. 'And let him get the evil out of you.'

'But there's nothing evil inside me!'

'That's what they all say,' said Professor Sydown. 'Now I shall begin.' He pointed the gun at Greta.

I looked at Percy and Grandpa Woebegone and

we nodded to each other. We did not have to say anything to know we were thinking the same thing.

As dreadful as Greta Woebegone was, she had called us her friends, and we were not going to let anything happen to her.

It was time to show these Spirit Smashers just how much smashing a spirit could actually do.

CHAPTER
16

'**R**elease this evil devil child from her torment!' shouted Professor Sydown at Greta, powering the gun up till it hummed.

Finally! Somebody else who thought the same about Greta as I did. Maybe this Professor Sydown wasn't as idiotic as I'd thought. I mean, she might be my friend, but she was still evil and definitely a devil child.

Greta gasped. 'Here, who are you calling "evil devil child"?'

'In sooth, I think he might be calling you an evil devil child, Greta,' Percy said. 'He's certainly looking your way.'

'Yes, thank you, Percy. I suspected he was talking about me,' Greta said with heroic patience. 'Now stop pointing that thing at me! Mother, tell him to stop!'

'I think it's for the best if you just let him get on with whatever he has to do, darling,' her mother said, her eyes alight with excitement.

And then Professor Sydown pulled the trigger.

A crackling filled the air and Greta's hair stood on end.

But that was it. It was all very dramatic but did not seem to be doing a huge amount.

'Doesn't look like we have much to worry about here,' Grandpa said. 'I reckon they are as useless as they look. No – *more* useless than they look.'

Unfortunately he was very wrong.

Greta looked at Grandpa in horror and yelped, 'I can't hear you!'

'WELL, WE SHALL SPEAK LOUDER THEN!' boomed Professor Sydown.

'Not you,' shouted Greta.

It looked like Professor Sydown had somehow managed to interfere with Greta's connection to the spirit world.

'Greta, can you hear me?' I asked, waving at her.

'I can see your lips moving but no sound is coming out,' she cried.

'THE SPIRITS MUST BE BLOCKING YOUR EARS!' Professor Sydown bellowed. 'WE SHALL SPEAK EVEN LOUDER!'

'Quickly,' I said to Percy and Grandpa. 'They are stopping Greta from hearing us! Soon she will not be able to talk to us! Or see us! We need to do something!'

'I shall get my poo stick!' said Percy.

'What possible use would that be?' I asked.

Percy's face creased in disappointment. 'I don't know! I just –'

'Do something! I can't hear what you're saying!' cried Greta, her eyes filling with tears.

'BEGONE, SPIRIT! UNBLOCK THIS CHILD'S EARS FROM THE EVIL FILLING THEM!' screamed

Professor Sydown at a volume that rattled the furniture.

Suddenly Percy jumped up and down. 'Grandpa Woebegone! Grandpa Woebegone! You can stop it!'

'How?' Grandpa Woebegone asked desperately.

'You can possess Professor Sydown!'

'Yes!' I shouted, amazed that Percy had somehow managed to hit on a good idea. 'Possess him!'

'Pass me the special incense, Chris,' said Professor Sydown, 'and let the smoke unblock this evil child's ears!'

Chris walked over to the equipment bag and started rummaging inside.

Grandpa Woebegone took a deep breath and set off running towards Professor Sydown.

Chris plucked a bottle out of the bag and began walking towards Professor Sydown.

And then slipped on the dead fish that nobody had thought to pick up.

He went careering forward, arms cartwheeling, into the arms of Professor Sydown, sending them both flying and the gun clattering to the floor, just

as Grandpa Woebegone jumped forward to dive into the body of Professor Sydown.

And shot into the body of Chris instead.

Professor Sydown and Chris ended up in a pile.

'Get off me, you blundering buffoon!' Professor Sydown shouted, struggling to push Chris off him.

'Oh, good grief!' said Chris/Grandpa Woebegone. 'I'm the wrong Spirit Smasher, aren't I? The dense one?'

'Yes, you are!' shouted Professor Sydown. 'Now get off me!'

'This really isn't very professional at all,' said Greta's mother through pursed lips, patting her purple hair.

'I can only apologize, Mrs Woebegone,' said Professor Sydown, managing to pull himself up off the floor. 'I assure you, this is not the performance you deserve. But we shall do better.'

'No, we won't,' said Chris/Grandpa Woebegone.

'Excuse me?!' asked Professor Sydown. 'We will!'

'No, we won't,' said Chris/Grandpa Woebegone. 'Because we are a big pair of useless wallies.'

'CHRISTOPHER!' snapped Professor Sydown. 'This is NO way for a Spirit Smasher to behave!'

'Well, it's true,' continued Chris/Grandpa Woebegone. 'You've *no* idea what you're doing.'

'How dare you?' cried Professor Sydown. 'I *do* know what I'm doing!'

'No, you don't. You're making it up as you go along,' Chris/Grandpa Woebegone said.

'So unprofessional!' tutted Greta's mother, crossing her arms.

'Oh, *you* can pipe down too!' snapped Chris/ Grandpa Woebegone. 'You Ribena-haired, yapping yogi!'

Prosecca gasped and her hands shot to her hair.

'CHRIS!' shouted Professor Sydown, whose eyes were nearly popping out of his head. 'WHAT ON EARTH HAS GOT INTO YOU?'

'Yes! Apologize to my wife this instant!' said Greta's father.

'And don't you start either!' said Chris/Grandpa Woebegone, pointing at Greta's father. 'If you want to get rid of the ghosts, why don't you read them some of your poetry? That'd be enough to drive anybody away!'

'CHRISTOPHER!' screamed Professor Sydown, who looked like steam was about to start blowing out of his ears. 'Stop talking IMMEDIATELY!'

'Oh, this is simply *wunderbar*!' I said, roaring with laughter.

'I can hear you again,' whooped Greta.

'It must have been when Chris bashed into Professor Sydown and knocked the gun out of his hands,' I said.

'Wonderful! That means I can leave this numbskull!' said Grandpa Woebegone, jumping out of Chris's body.

Chris staggered backwards and shook his head. Now back in possession of his own body, he stood in the middle of the room, a look of intense bafflement across his already pretty baffled-looking face, wondering why Professor Sydown and Greta's parents were all staring at him with looks of utter fury.

'What?' Chris said innocently. 'Why are you all looking at me like that?'

Prosecca Woebegone drew a deep breath. 'GET! OUT! OF! MY! HOUSE! THIS! INSTANT!'

CHAPTER 17

An hour or two of intense mollifying later, Professor Sydown had finally calmed Greta's mother and begged her to give them another chance. Realizing she had no one else to turn to if the Spirit Smashers failed, she had given in and recanted her previous banishing.

Greta was in her room, chatting to Percy. I had snuck in through the floorboards under her bed, which is not as weird as it sounds and was absolutely not spying. I was merely gathering information for this little tale.

'And verily that's how I won the village Push-a-Poo Brown Crown two years in a row,' Percy said proudly.

'How fascinating!' Greta said without much enthusiasm. 'Percy, tell me more about your life.'

''Twas very ordinary really,' Percy began. 'It was just like yours, I'm sure. Earning a groat or two by helping to bury plague victims. Throwing turnips at the old men of the village. Witch burnings on a Saturday morning . . .' Percy let out a long sigh. 'Such happy times.'

His face darkened. 'But then the Black Death came for my family. And I died too. And now with no one to remember me I might as well never have existed.'

'That's terrible,' said Greta. 'Your whole family.'

'Yes, it was so hard watching them go. But worse knowing they are somewhere else and I can't get there. All I want to do is to join them. But I'm stuck here in this house. I can't leave. I can't seem to pass to the other side. I don't know why.'

Greta was beginning to think she knew exactly why Percy couldn't pass. And better than that, she was beginning to think she knew how to help him. But before she did, she had to make sure the Spirit

Smashers left and never came back.

'And how are you going to do *that*, child?' I asked.

Greta and Percy both jumped.

'Would you *stop* creeping around like that?' said Greta.

'I do not "creep"! I simply slide into rooms unnoticed.'

'That sounds *exactly* like creeping to me.'

I will concede she might have had a tiny point.

A short while later, everybody had gathered in the sitting room once again. Chris and Professor Sydown were in full black boiler suits with the Spirit Smashers emblem and looked ready for action.

'We will *definitely* do it this time,' said Professor Sydown with a level of confidence that not one other person in the room, dead or alive, shared. 'Or my name isn't Professor Sydown. Isn't that right, Chris?'

'N-yes! I mean, yes!' Chris replied. 'We'll definitely get rid of

BUZZZZZZ

them this time, Missus Woebegone.
No more mistakes.'

'Hmm,' hmmed Greta's mother
with narrowed eyes.

The Spirit Smashers
started setting their equipment
up all around the house
– little black boxes with flashing lights
and antennae on top, and screens and
keyboards, which they fiddled with for
the longest time.

Our fear turned into boredom. Larry lay on the floor, sucking on a lorry like a pipe. Greta's father even fell asleep in his chair and only woke when his pipe dropped out of his mouth, spilling hot ash all over his lap. He yelped and brushed it off on to the carpet, to tuts from his wife and glares from Professor Sydown.

'Very sorry,' said Greta's father. 'Do continue.'

And on they continued.

The piano stared at me from the corner of the room.

I stared back.

The piano stared back at me again.

I stared back harder.

It was very dramatic.

'Why are you staring so hard at the piano?' asked Grandpa Woebegone. 'Looks like you're a sandwich short of a picnic.'

I had no idea why he was suggesting a picnic, so I ignored that and merely answered his question.

'None of your business, old man who smells weird.'

'Look,' Grandpa said, nodding at the piano, 'if you want to play the bally thing, just play it! What harm can it do?'

'You don't understand,' I said. 'I . . . cannot.'

'You know, I said "cannot" too many times in my life,' said Grandpa Woebegone, a great sadness in his eyes. 'Every one of them I regret. Fear does you no good.'

'Go on,' said Percy, who had crept up beside me. 'Play the piano.'

I closed my eyes. Maybe it was time for me to face my fear. No one could ever say that Wolfgang van Bach-Storey was a coward. We still needed to spook the Spirit Smashers, and what could be more terrifying than the sound of beautiful piano music being played by invisible unearthly fingers . . .

I slid over to the piano.

I used my powers to open the lid.

I placed my fingers on the keys, finally feeling once again the ivory beneath them. My palms were sweating – or would have been, if I was not a ghost.

I took a deep breath and began to play.

Everyone in the room stopped what they were doing and gasped.

I played the first few notes, joy flowing through me as I once more created beauty –

'What is that hellish racket?' said Professor Sydown. 'Never have I heard such a nightmarish noise.'

How dare he?! I could not believe such rudeness.

'I may be a little out of practice,' I said in my defence.

'Such amateur spectral piano,' moaned Professor Sydown, putting his hands over his ears. 'It must be the ghost of a child playing – perhaps even a toddler bashing the keys.'

OUTRAGE UPON OUTRAGE! A '*TODDLER*'?

Never in all the years of my life – and death – had I heard such monstrous mudslinging!

And my so-called friends, Greta and Grandpa Woebegone and Percy, just stood there, their silence deafening.

I would take my revenge upon this man if it were the last thing I did. I slammed shut the piano lid and stormed out of the sitting room, not looking at anybody.

I slunk down to my cellar and petted Ludwig for a while.

'Oh, little Ludwig! Sweet little Ludwig! You are my one true friend, the love of my life.'

'It is a little disturbing,' squeaked Ludwig. 'That

you, a grown man, just over two hundred years old, are best friends with a rat. You should get out more.'

Ludwig was so funny! I never stopped laughing with him. He knows full well I cannot 'get out more'.

'You really need to make more friends and stop bothering me all the time,' he squeaked kindly, always thinking of me.

He was right, though. I *should* find new friends. But in *this* house? No. Greta, Grandpa Woebegone and Percy were laughing at my misfortune upstairs, I was sure of it. I did not wish to face their giggling mockery. I did not wish to think of their betrayal. This time I was ashamed to say I wept.

A short while later, a voice startled me.

'Hi there,' said Greta.

I quickly wiped my eyes. 'What do *you* want?'

'I just wanted to see if you were OK?' Greta gave me a small smile.

Grandpa Woebegone and Percy had floated in behind her.

'What do *you* care?'

'Of course we care,' said Greta, and the other two nodded in agreement.

'Well, I'm FINE, *danke* very much!' I said, crossing my arms and looking away from the treacherous trio.

'You don't seem fine,' said Grandpa Woebegone. 'And look – you've soaked Ludwig.'

Percy shuddered at the sight of Ludwig and stepped backwards. 'Keep that rat away from me!'

I looked down at little Ludwig. I had, without realizing, been using him to wipe my tear-stained face, and now his fur was very soggy. Poor Ludwig. Poor Wolfgang.

Ludwig gazed up at me, his eyes full of pity. 'Put. Me. Down,' he squeaked.

I placed him down carefully.

'*Unbelievable*,' he squeaked, skittering away.

Sweet little rat – he knew he had done all he could to help me. I sat in silence, trying to ignore the others.

'I'm sorry about what Professor Sydown said about your piano playing,' said Greta.

'So sorry you said nothing to defend my honour!'
I harrumphed.

'You didn't give me a chance before you flounced
out.'

I gasped, hand to my chest. 'I did not flounce
out! I *stormed* out!'

'OK. Stormed out. Well, anyway – I loved hearing
you play the piano,' said Greta. 'It was beautiful.'

'Pah!' I said with the appropriate amount of sneer
in my voice. What did Greta Woebegone know? She

was just a child. 'You heard what the professor said! He thought a child – *nein*, a *toddler* – was playing!'

Grandpa Woebegone walked up to me and put his arm round my shoulder. I tried shrugging it off, but he put it back. 'You have to remember, Wolfgang, those people upstairs are idiots. They don't know what they are talking about.'

What he said was true. They *were* idiots. How could common people like them possibly understand the music I had played? They were no better than the turnip farmers that worked the fields outside of Smackenzibotten.

A smile crossed my face unbidden. I would not let Professor Sydown crush me. No – *I* would crush *him*! It was time to somehow get rid of the Spirit Smashers for good.

By the time we all rushed back upstairs, though, the pair had finished setting up their equipment and testing it.

Professor Sydown collapsed on the sofa, putting a hand on his brow. 'I am exhausted. The battle with the spirits has worn me out today. But we shall return tomorrow, well rested, and rid this house of demons once and for all.'

'Tomorrow afternoon, though,' reminded Chris. 'Don't forget, I'm volunteering at the zoo in the morning. There's an elephant with diarrhoea I need to look after.'

'Fine!' said Professor Sydown, a look of exasperation on his face. 'We shall return tomorrow *afternoon*. And then the war against the Woebegone ghosts will at last be won!'

Well, we would see about that.

The Battle of Woebegone Hall *would* finish tomorrow – but not as this nincompoop expected . . .

CHAPTER 18

The Woebegone family did not sleep well that night. Greta's mother and father had terrible nightmares that had them tossing and turning.

Fine – I admit it! I crept into their rooms and whispered dark dreams into their ears as they slept. It is another of my talents and amuses me endlessly.

I made Greta's father dream he was tiny and being chased by huge mice. I made Greta's mother

dream she was huge but being chased by a horde of tiny snapping crocodiles.

It was so much fun watching them squirm in terror as they slept.

I did not give Greta nightmares, though – she had her own to battle with.

I slipped into her mind and saw her fears.

Her grandmother gone. The Woebegone ghosts all gone. And Greta left completely alone.

In the house.

Forever.

A bicycle wheel spinning endlessly.

The family awoke the next day with groggy heads to face the long, nervous wait until Professor Sydown and Chris arrived.

Greta, of course, first went to say good morning to her grandmother, who – surprise upon surprise – was in bed. Rather more unexpectedly Grandpa was there too, sitting in the chair in the corner of the room.

Grandma looked, if anything, even frailer as

she patted the bed. 'Come and sit next to your old grandma, Greta,' she said.

Greta fell on to the bed and curled up next to her grandmother. The sun had broken through the cloud outside, and shafts of cold sunlight broke into the room through the grimy window. The shadows of the last autumn leaves shivered on the bedspread.

'You are looking pale,' Grandma said to Greta.

And it was true. Greta's skin was the colour of the dawn snow blanketing the worm field.

'Have you been outside yet?' Grandma asked.

'Not yet, Grandma,' Greta replied. 'Soon.'

I could feel it, though.

Her lie.

And, behind it all, her memories.

Her fear.

Her heart pounding at the thought of stepping outside.

Greta pushed the thoughts away and said, 'Grandma, tell me – what was it like being a racing driver?'

'Well, it was noisy for one thing,' laughed

Grandma. 'The sound of the car – sheesh, it went right through you. Even though you plugged your ears, you could still feel it. And the smell. It was . . . how to describe it . . . ? It smelled of anticipation. It smelled of *heaven*. I think the moments before a race started, the steering wheel vibrating in my hand, waiting for the flag . . . I think they were the happiest moments of my life. Along with all the times I spent with your grandpa, of course,' she added, her face softening into a distant smile.

I could see Grandpa's face crumple slightly at that, a mix of pain and happiness etched on his face.

'And soon we'll be reunited. On the other side.'

'But, Grandma, Grandpa hasn't passed to the other side yet. He's sitting right there,' Greta said, pointing.

Grandma turned to look in the direction of Grandpa. 'And you'll go when the time is right, won't you, darling?'

Grandpa sat there looking helpless, for once saying nothing.

The nerves increased and hardly a further word was spoken that day before the sound of the Spirit Smashers van pulling up, followed by the ringing of the doorbell, broke the silence.

When Professor Sydown and Chris entered the house they had a new air of seriousness about them.

They looked in no mood for messing as they unpacked the black Spirit Smashers bag and laid out more baffling, flashing, beeping equipment – but this time also candles, holy water and a great scroll sealed with wax.

'The Scroll of Abolishment,' Professor Sydown announced solemnly as he placed it gently on the table.

'The Candle of Banishment,' he announced solemnly as he placed a huge candle next to the scroll.

'The Sandwich of Egg,' said Chris, carefully laying his lunchbox on the table.

The Spirit Smashers put on their boiler suits again, together with goggles and big rubber gloves, which I had to admit was rather intimidating. I gave a small gulp, and felt a shiver run through me.

A foul smell began to spread through the room, thick and choking.

Greta's mother held her nose and wafted her hand in front of her.

'Good grief,' said Greta's father. 'What is that stench?'

'Evil spirits,' said his wife knowledgeably.

'Egg sandwich more like,' muttered Greta.

'Sadly not,' said Professor Sydown glaring at Chris. 'Well! Go on then, tell them!' he snapped.

'I'm afraid that might be me, Mr and Mrs Woebegone.' Chris blushed. 'I had early-morning duty at the zoo. First, I had to muck out the buffalo enclosure. Then I had to scrub the walruses. And then I had to collect a urine sample from a very angry gorilla with a very bad aim.'

'And after all that,' said Professor Sydown, 'what did you forget to do?'

'Take a shower, Professor Sydown,' replied Chris, looking down at his shoes. 'Really sorry, Mr and Mrs Woebegone.'

'Over an hour to drive here with that . . . unholy aroma. I thought I was going to faint,' said Professor Sydown. 'The van will never smell the same again. But if we can all *please* try to ignore it and get on with the job at hand. This house is still riddled with spirits and today *shall* be the day they are banished.'

And then Professor Sydown and Chris began.

They turned on all the little boxes dotted around the house.

'To lock the psychic energy and transmute it

from this world to the next,' explained Professor Sydown.

They then lit candles in every room.

'To control the spirits,' explained Professor Sydown.

They then burned incense, the heady aroma making us all feel a little weak.

'To get rid of the stench of fishy walrus and buffalo poo,' explained Chris, shamefaced.

'Right,' Greta's mother said with a face of thunder. 'You. Upstairs. Shower, now.'

A short while later, Chris took his place again next to Professor Sydown, his hair dripping wet but the smell in the house greatly lessened.

Professor Sydown and Chris started fiddling with all sorts of buttons and knobs until a humming shot through the house, electricity throbbing through all the little black boxes.

The vibrations made my head ache, and, by the looks of Percy and Grandpa, it was doing the same to them. Professor Sydown ran around, pressing

more and more buttons until suddenly a beam of energy shot from box to box, lighting up the whole house in green.

The light crackled and fizzed.

My head screamed.

Professor Sydown, sweat pouring down his brow, twisted more dials. The beam became brighter and brighter until, as one, with a final crackling bang, the little boxes exploded.

Professor Sydown fell backwards on to the sofa, panting with exhaustion. 'Woebegone family – this house is clean!'

'Thank you very much,' said Greta's mother. 'I have an excellent lady who comes twice a week.'

'No! I mean, this house is clean of ghosts! They have been cast out. They are no more!'

'Really?' asked Greta's mother, eyeing Professor Sydown suspiciously.

Really? We ghosts shrugged at each other. We were all still very much there.

'Yes. The foul spirits have been sent on from this world to the next,' Professor Sydown said. 'You

can finally be at peace, Woebegone family. After you have paid me in full.'

'Professor Sydown?' asked Greta's father, pointing his pipe. 'Why is our cat floating?'

Professor Sydown swung round to see Pussy Lanimous was indeed floating behind his head.

'Gah!' Professor Sydown yelped and jumped into the air.

And then slowly, following the cat, Larry floated into the room, clutching a lorry.

Greta glared at me. Grandpa glared at me. Even Percy was glaring at me. *Why* were they glaring at me? I could not understand. Was my little joke not an amusing one?

And then I realized. If only I had not done my little joke, we could have pretended the Spirit Smashers had succeeded!

All I had done was alert them – and Greta's parents – to the fact that we were still there.

Stupid Wolfgang!

I looked apologetically at Greta. She gave me a small smile of forgiveness, which I am ashamed to admit filled my heart with what can only be described as happiness (which when I realized what

it was, made me shudder in disgust).

I then let Pussy Lanimous go, who tore off out of the room in terror. I slowly placed Larry on the floor. He did not tear off in terror, but threw his lorry and hit Chris on the forehead.

'Do you have ANY idea at all what you're doing, Sydown?' asked Greta's father. 'Because I really don't believe you do. And I think it's time you left our house. *Without* payment.'

Greta's mother nodded vigorously in agreement.

I looked at Greta, whose eyes were full of hope.

Could it have been so easy? Had we rid ourselves of the Spirit Smashers? Would we be left in peace?

No such luck.

'No!' exclaimed Professor Sydown. 'The spirits are tricksy and deceiving. Please, give us one more chance! One final chance, when we will use every single power at our disposal!'

Professor Sydown held his hands together, as if he were praying.

Greta's parents looked at each other.

Her mother held up one finger. 'One last

chance,' she said. 'That's it. And then you're out. Agreed?'

'Agreed,' said Professor Sydown.

Chris whooped and held his hand up for what I believe is called a 'high-five', but Professor Sydown merely glared and left him hanging, which is the highest of all bad manners.

The Spirit Smashers set about repairing the equipment that had exploded. An hour later, the boxes started humming again and crackling light shot between them.

'Now,' said Professor Sydown, 'we shall show no mercy. Christopher, pass me the Scroll of Abolishment!'

Chris let out a gasp of horror. 'Are you sure, Professor?'

'Yes! Pass it to me!'

'Because the last time you used that, you got possessed by the ghost of a small child and weed your boiler suit –'

'PASS ME THE SCROLL OF ABOLISHMENT!'

Chris quickly passed Professor Sydown the

Scroll of Abolishment.

'Christopher, light the Candle of Banishment!'

Chris gasped again. 'Are you absolutely sure about that, Professor?'

'Yes.'

'Because the last time you used the Scroll of Abolishment and the Candle of Banishment at the same time you got possessed by a spider and started eating flies and –'

'ENOUGH! LIGHT THE CANDLE!'

Chris lit the candle, and the moment the flame flickered alive, the electricity between the boxes started crackling even more fiercely and the strangest feeling overtook me. It was almost as if the longer the candle burned, the weaker I felt. By the looks on the faces of the other ghosts, they were feeling the same sensation.

'Remember, Christopher,' said Professor Sydown, 'under no circumstances let this candle go out. Now! Spirits, begone!' Professor shouted, his arms aloft. 'Leave this house! Leave the Woebegone family in peace!'

Chris, standing next to Professor Sydown, held his arms aloft too, and bellowed, 'Leave the Woebegone family in peace! The power of Chris compels you! The power of Chris compels you!'

Professor Sydown then broke the red wax seal on the Scroll of Abolishment, cleared his throat and started reading.

Immediately I felt a heavy tiredness upon me – as if all I wanted to do was fall asleep and never wake up.

Percy dropped to the floor. Grandpa Woebegone staggered.

Greta looked at us in horror. She knew straight away that we were in big trouble.

The more Professor Sydown read from the Scroll of Abolishment, the more tired we became.

'Possess the professor!' I shouted at Grandpa, but he shook his head. Already he was too weak.

As the candle burned on, I felt my un-life slipping away.

I saw myself slowly begin to disappear, as if I were smoke, floating away into nothingness.

It was highly unpleasant.

I could see Percy, groaning, begin to disappear too. His hands were disintegrating, and he looked at them in terror. Grandpa Woebegone's feet were dissolving, and he fell to his knees.

Greta jumped up.

'Sit down, Greta!' barked her mother.

'But, Mother, you don't understand –'

'I do! And it ends right now, so SIT DOWN!'

Greta looked at me in misery, despair etched on her face. 'Please,' she said to me. 'Do something. You have to!'

We had to somehow put the cursed candle out! I tried crawling towards it but collapsed. I was too weak to poltergeist. Grandpa Woebegone was in no state to possess anybody. Percy was more useless than ever, if that is imaginable.

We were done for. Defeated. This was my lowest point since farming worms.

I looked down and there, by my feet, I saw a familiar face. Little Ludwig, his nose twitching. My greatest friend had come to say goodbye.

But then I saw something that chilled me to my bone. His adorable little tail was disappearing. That could only mean one thing. Ludwig was a ghost, just like me. And that meant if I did not do something, Ludwig would also die forever. I could not bear the thought!

'My poor Ludwig! Come and sit with me as we share our final moments together,' I said sadly.

'Or,' squeaked Ludwig, 'you could get off your bony butt and do something about it?'

I gave Ludwig a sad smile. 'A fool's hope, my sweet ratty friend.'

There was nothing that could be done. It was the end.

'You need to blow the candle out!' said Ludwig.

'I no longer have the breath in my lungs,' I wheezed as I closed my eyes.

'Then don't use your lungs,' squeaked Ludwig. 'Remember your final performance at the palace . . .'

My eyes sprang open. But of course! There was more than one way to blow out a candle.

I crawled across the floor, every inch like torture.

I reached the sofa and, as if I were reaching the top of a mountain, I pulled myself up. Finally I could rid myself of the demons of my past and the terrible memory of that fateful night. Redemption was in my grasp.

I angled my bottom towards the Candle of Banishment and, with the last ounce of my dying strength, I blasted a great fart towards it.

CHAPTER 19

I had assumed, of course, that ghostly farts would not be flammable, and that my poltergeist parp would simply blow out the candle.

Alas, it was not so.

As soon as the gassy fart touched the candle, it erupted into a fierce jet of flames.

And woe upon woe! Terrible double misfortune! Once again my blazing fart hit a curtain.

The flames started licking at the curtain, spreading like . . . spreading like . . . fire! In an instant it jumped from the curtains to the carpet and even to the bookshelf. Everybody stood staring in horror at the unfolding conflagration.

I was frozen in terror, my mind back in the

palace on that terrible, accursed night.

It had happened again. My bottom had caused another disastrous inferno.

No! I could not let history repeat itself! But what could I do?

And then I spied the huge bottle of holy water on the table.

I had no strength to lift it but what if I could possess someone? If a ghost as unimpressive as Grandpa Woebegone could possess people, surely I could manage it too?

I staggered to my feet and, with a hidden reserve of strength I did not believe I had, ran towards Chris and jumped into his body.

It worked! I was in control of Chris!

I grabbed the bottle, unscrewed it and started throwing the contents all over the curtains, carpet and bookshelf. I threw it all around the room, accidentally spraying Greta's parents and Professor Sydown.

The flames died down and then fizzled out.

The moment the last flame was extinguished, I jumped back out of Chris.

I was back to full strength, and by the looks of Grandpa Woebegone and Percy, who were both getting back on their feet, they were fine too.

'Oh, Wolfgang,' said Greta, her face glowing with happiness. 'You've saved everybody. You're a hero.'

I felt my heart would burst with joy. For the first time since that night at the palace I was truly happy. I even thought for a moment that my eyes had filled with tears, but then I realized they were just smarting from something noxious in the air.

'Good *grief*,' said Greta's mother. '*What* is that awful smell?'

'Ugh,' said Greta, holding her nose and her breath too. 'It's terrible!'

'It smells like . . .' said Professor Sydown. 'I can't put my finger on it . . . It smells like . . . OH NO!'

He grabbed the bottle of holy water that Chris was still clutching and sniffed it carefully.

'UGHHH! NOOO!' he cried, recoiling as if slapped. 'Chris! Might it be possible at the zoo this morning that you got the bottle of holy water and the bottle of . . . gorilla wee mixed up?'

Oopsie.

'ARE YOU SAYING,' boomed Prosecca Woebegone, puffing herself up to her considerable height, her purple hair dripping wet, like a bewigged angry scorpion who has just had the worst shower of its life, 'ARE YOU SAYING THAT YOU HAVE JUST DRENCHED MY SITTING ROOM IN GORILLA WEE?'

Double oopsie.

Having been possessed by me at the time, Chris clearly had no memory of throwing the wee around the room. He stood staring at the bottle he was still holding, then at Greta's mother, then back at the bottle, the look in his eyes slowly turning from confusion to panic. I almost felt sorry for him. Almost.

'But-but-but . . .' he stammered.

'Don't "but" the woman!' shouted Professor Sydown. 'Answer her!'

All Chris could do was slowly nod.

At that all hell broke loose.

Greta's mother let out a howl of rage. Her father threw his pipe at Professor Sydown. Professor Sydown had picked up a cloth and was trying to wipe Greta's mother down, but she grabbed the Scroll of Abolishment and started hitting Chris with it.

'RIGHT!' she roared. 'BOTH OF YOU, GET OUT OF MY HOUSE! THIS INSTANT!'

'Please, Mrs Woebegone!' pleaded Professor Sydown. 'One last chance!'

A few sharp raps round the head with the Scroll of Abolishment convinced Professor Sydown any hopes of a last chance he might have had were in vain.

'GET OUT OF HERE, YOU SENSELESS, SQUIRREL-BRAINED SPIRIT SMASHERS!' Greta's mother yelled, raining more bashes from the Scroll of Abolishment on the heads of the hapless twosome. 'GET OUT, YOU PAIR OF PRATTLING PARANORMAL PUDDING-HEADS!'

Professor Sydown and Chris ran around trying to gather their belongings as Greta's mother chased after them, hitting them with the scroll again and again. Meanwhile, Greta's father bashed them with his wheelchair and hurled books at the two horrified Spirit Smashers. Finally Professor Sydown and Chris ran out of the house, screaming in terror.

Greta's mother stood in the centre of the sitting room panting, still clutching the Scroll of Abolishment, which had certainly succeeded in driving unwanted visitors out of the house, just not in the way the Spirit Smashers had intended. Then she collapsed backwards on to the sofa.

Silence draped the sitting room, apart from the sound of Larry pushing his lorry through the puddles of gorilla wee.

'So,' Greta's mother said, turning to her husband, 'what are we going to do now?'

'I think,' said Greta's father, solemnly packing his pipe with tobacco, 'we have to learn when we're beat.'

'So we just give up?'

'Darling, look around.'

Greta's mother gazed at the devastation caused by the Spirit Smashers.

She let out a great sigh. 'I suppose you're right.'

Greta shot me a huge grin and gave me a thumbs up. I gave her the thumbs up back. Grandpa Woebegone and Percy gave each other a great hug.

We had won.

Greta's mother stood and slowly started cleaning up the mess.

'I'm never going to get my yoga studio, am I?'

The first thing Greta did, of course, was run upstairs to see her grandma. She flopped excitedly next to her on her bed.

'We did it, Grandma! Grandpa is safe! All the ghosts are safe.'

'That's wonderful news!' Grandma Woebegone

said, putting down her knitting.

'So everything is perfect and you're not going anywhere!' said Greta, beaming.

'Not yet anyway,' Grandma said, patting Greta's hand.

'Yes, and – hang on. What do you mean "not yet"?' Greta asked, her brow furrowing.

'I suppose I mean that I won't be here forever. Grandpa will be moving on soon and I intend to join him.'

Greta's lip wobbled. 'Don't say that!'

'You'll remember me, though, won't you? So it's not like I'll be completely gone. I will live on here,' she said, tapping on Greta's chest.

Greta nodded, not trusting her own voice.

Grandpa walked into the room and sat next to Greta on the bed.

'And I'll have him to keep me company,' Grandma said, nodding at Grandpa.

'We'll be back together very soon,' Grandpa Woebegone replied softly. 'I do love you. More than you'll ever know.'

'You . . . love Grandma?' Greta said, uncertainly.

'Of course he does!' Grandma Woebegone said, nodding.

'Yes, but . . . ' Greta struggled to find the right words. 'He hasn't exactly shown it in the past.'

Grandpa looked at Grandma, his eyes filled with tears. 'It was those blasted Spirit Smashers. When I was on the floor, and I thought I was done for, the only thing in my mind keeping me going was Grandma. It took nearly dying – for a second time – to remember she means everything to me. I'm nothing without her,' he said, his voice breaking.

'I know, my darling,' Grandma Woebegone said, with a soft smile.

Greta gasped. 'Hang on – you can hear Grandpa? Can you see him?'

Grandma smiled. 'Yes, of course I can see him! He's right there,' she said, pointing straight at him.

'She really can now, Greta,' said Grandpa Woebegone.

'But . . . how?' Greta asked, mystified.

'I'm not sure. But perhaps it's because she is that much closer to the other side. Her time to pass over is soon. Very soon . . .'

Greta's tears fell freely down her face. 'No! You can't both go!'

'We are old,' Grandma Woebegone said. 'And your grandpa and I have spent too long apart. It's time we were together again,' Grandma said. 'Finally.'

'But I have one last thing to do before I leave,' said Grandpa mysteriously.

A short while later, Grandpa found Greta, in a white dress bright against the slate sky, sat looking out of the glass doors of the conservatory. Rain was drumming on the roof and running rivers down the windows.

Greta was feeling very sorry for herself. She looked at Grandpa, her face pale.

Ghostly.

'Hello, Grandpa,' she said.

'Hello, love. You look wetter than the weather.'

'Please don't leave,' she said plainly.

'Greta, it's my time. I'm excited to move on. I need to have one final adventure. With your grandma.' He kneeled beside Greta and looked into her eyes. 'And it's time for you to get your life back too.'

Greta shook her head.

'Greta, it's time to go outside again,' he said a little more firmly.

She shook her head again. 'I can't,' she said in a tiny voice. 'I'm too scared.' She squeezed her eyes shut tightly.

'Greta, you may be scared, but you are also brave.'

'I'm not!'

'Oh, you are! Far braver that I will ever be! You have faced ghosts. You have faced your parents. You have even faced death. And you are still full of life. I lived my life so full of fear. I made Grandma give up the thing she loved most because *I* was frightened. I didn't go off and see the world. I was a fool! And that's what fear can cause,' Grandpa said. 'A lifetime of regret. And you've helped show me this.

269

Now I can move on – ridding myself of fear has released me. So now it's your turn, Greta. Go. Go and live your life. Outside.'

Greta said nothing but nodded once, stood up and slowly walked to the glass doors. Her heart was in her mouth and she felt faint.

'Go on!' urged Grandpa. 'You can do it!'

She placed a hand on the doorknob, turned it and opened the two doors. Her knees were weak.

'That's it!' whispered Grandpa.

And then, for the first time since the dreadful day of the accident, Greta Woebegone stepped outside the house.

She turned to Grandpa and beamed, and he gave her a thumbs up.

She walked out into the garden, into the rain. She closed her eyes, her face glistening wet, her dress darkening. She held her arms to the sky and laughed.

I watched as she started running, jumping and dancing in the pouring rain.

My heart ached; how I yearned to once

again feel the rain. How long had it been since I had felt the crunch of autumn leaves under my feet? How long since I had felt the warmth of the sun on my skin? How long since I had breathed in fresh cold air or felt the brush of wet snowflakes on my cheeks?

Too long. Too long.

But no. These things were not for poor Wolfgang.

I was not destined to go outside. I belonged to the house.

And the house belonged to me.

Percy walked into the conservatory and stood next to Grandpa.

'Forsooth, is she all right in the head?' Percy asked, nodding at Greta, who was lying on the ground, waving her arms and legs in the air.

'She is now,' replied Grandpa.

I stood next to them. Three ghosts together. But not for long.

'It's time for me to go,' Grandpa said. 'I can feel it. I'm finally ready.'

Percy and I nodded solemnly but didn't say anything.

'Tell Greta I said goodbye. I don't think I can,'
Grandpa said, his voice choked. 'Turns out there
are some things I'm still frightened of. Damn fool.
But tell her I love her very much. Tell her she is my
inspiration. And tell her to remember me.'

We nodded again.

'Goodbye, you two,' he said, and Percy gave
him a tearful hug. 'Wolfgang, you're crying!' lied
Grandpa. What a huge liar he was! 'You are, after
all, a good man.'

Grandpa gave a final smile and walked out. I wiped my face, blew my nose on my sleeve, and secretly followed him.

He went upstairs to Grandma's room and I spied him through the keyhole.

No, not spied. *Observed*.

Grandpa Woebegone placed his hand on his wife's hand and bent down to kiss her, not quite touching either her hand or her cheek. 'I'll wait for you on the other side,' he said. 'See you soon, my love.'

I pulled my eye away from the keyhole. Sometimes one has to know when to stop observing and leave the story alone. And that was the final time I – or anybody else – saw Grandpa Woebegone.

A little while later, Greta bustled back into the house, her dress covered in mud, her hair hanging in wet tresses like sweet little Ludwig's tail, her face flushed with colour.

'I did it!' she blurted, out of breath. 'Where's Grandpa? I want to thank him!'

'Ah,' I said. 'Teeny-tiny problem there.'

'What?' she asked.

'He's gone.'

'What do you mean "he's gone"?'

'I mean, he's passed to the other side.'

'Just like that?' Greta fell on to the sofa. 'Did he say anything?'

'*Ja,*' I said. 'He said –' and it was then I realized I had forgotten his message – 'goodbye.'

'That was it?'

'No . . . he also said . . . give up the recorder. And don't be rude to Wolfgang. That's what he said.'

Greta looked at me with deep suspicion. And then she ran upstairs to her grandmother.

I left them to it. I had seen quite enough tears for one day.

The next morning, the sound of hammering could be heard from the garden. I peered out through the condensation on the window. Between frozen grey skies and a colourless landscape, Greta was kneeling in the soil, hammering two small planks of wood together.

When she finished hammering, she got out what looked like an old man's pocket knife, and started carving. What she was carving – or whose name – I could not see. It was too far away.

But I guessed.

'Percy,' Greta said when she came back in and found Percy in my cellar, 'I want you to see something.'

Percy gave her a look of curiosity and followed her to the kitchen window.

She pointed to the cross, now standing at the end of the garden.

'That's for you,' she said. 'Your very own grave. With your name on it.'

Percy's hand went to his mouth. He said nothing, just stared.

'I will look after it,' said Greta. 'And when I'm older, I will get you a proper gravestone in the family graveyard. And it will say "Percy Woebegone. Witch-scarer. Stick-Push-a-Poo Champion. And Great Friend. Forever missed. Never forgotten".'

Percy looked at Greta and whispered, so quietly

I could hardly hear, 'I'm not a no-body any more. I'm a some-body. Thank you.'

'Shall we go out and lay flowers on it?'

Percy nodded.

Out they walked into the garden, but of course I could not follow.

I watched them, though, as Greta laid flowers by the wooden cross.

Perfect white snow began to fall, and Percy began to fade, until he too was gone forever.

And that left one last ghost.

CHAPTER 20

Greta found me in the cellar cradling sweet little Ludwig.

'That is quite enough cradling, Wolfgang,' squeaked Ludwig. 'It's not dignified. For either of us.'

I placed Ludwig on the grimy floor.

'You know,' he squeaked, 'you *really* need to get out more.'

It was true. But I could not.

'Hello, Wolfgang,' Greta said, her face red and blotchy.

I did not reply. I knew why she had come.

'You're the last ghost,' she said. 'The others have both passed over to the other side. They are at peace.'

I still said nothing.

'I don't know what *you* want, though, Wolfgang. What would make you happy?'

It was Ludwig who had put the idea in my head.

'I would very much like to play the piano.'

'Well then, let's do it!' said Greta.

I gasped. 'I cannot,' I said.

I thought back to the calamity at the palace. The cruel words of the Spirit Smashers about my playing. Every time I thought of the piano, a flash of pain seared my mind.

'Because I'm frightened,' I said in a tiny voice.

Me! The great and terrifying Wolfgang van Bach-Storey, who had once performed in front of royalty! Frightened as a tiny mouse! Unimaginable!

But true.

'Come on,' said Greta. She smiled at me and I knew I would trust that smile forever. 'It's time for you to face your fear.'

I nodded, terror gripping my heart. I placed sweet little Ludwig in my pocket and walked up the stairs and into the sitting room, as if walking to my own execution. I sat upon the piano stool, the music swimming before my eyes.

I closed my eyes and breathed deeply, then I began to play.

And it was as if I had never stopped. The centuries disappeared, and it was as if I were once again performing in front of an audience of thousands. I could remember it all, every single note.

In came Mr and Mrs Woebegone, Larry and even

Pussy Lanimous, and they stood in rapt silence, listening. The music flowed through me and out to them.

I am not ashamed to say that I wept as my fingers danced across the keys, so beautiful was the feeling to play music again.

I played on and on into the evening, until it was just Greta, Ludwig and me left in the room. Finally I played the final note and closed the piano lid, my heart filled with joy. And then I sensed myself fading. I could feel myself leaving this world, the other side pulling at me.

'Goodbye, dear Wolfgang,' Greta said, her voice as soft and quiet as falling snow. 'It's your time.'

But no.

Not yet.

Soon but not yet.

Greta had already lost too much.

And besides – I was having far too much fun down here.

'No, my evil devil child,' I whispered for old times' sake. 'I shall not be leaving just yet. I think you might need me around, just for a little while longer.'

'Because you're my friend, Wolfgang? And you care about me?'

'What? No! Absolutely not because of *that*.'

'Wolfgang. I know I'm right.'

'Fine! Whatever. *Maybe* I'm your friend. Don't make such a big deal of it.'

And that leaves one final scene for me to recount before I say goodbye – for now.

Greta was once again in her favourite place in the whole world – her grandmother's bedroom. Just one week had passed since the Woebegone ghosts – Grandpa and Percy – had gone to the other side, and yet already it seemed like Grandma Woebegone was even more frail.

Greta was spending every possible moment with her, trying to carefully remember every tiny detail. She had even managed to take her out in a wheelchair, down the high street to the shops. They had both arrived back flushed and happy, Grandma Woebegone still beaming at the thought of all the people who remembered her and shouted 'Hello, Mildred!' as Greta pushed her down the street.

But now Grandma was back in her bed, exhausted.

'There's something I want you to have,' she said. 'Under the bed.'

'It's not your snail farm, is it?' asked Greta.

Grandma Woebegone smiled and shook her head. 'It's in the big wooden box at the back.'

Greta ducked down and rummaged around until she found the box and pulled it out. She sat back on the bed and opened it.

Inside, gleaming as if it were still brand new, was Grandma's racing helmet. It was bright purple with silver trim, and the most beautiful thing Greta had ever seen.

'Are you sure?' Greta asked, eyes wide.

'Go on! Try it on!' Grandma urged.

Greta didn't wait to be told twice. She pulled it on to her head and tightened the strap.

'It fits perfectly!' Grandma said. 'Now go and ride your bike.'

Greta took a moment, then jumped up. 'Thank you, Grandma!' Then she bounded down the stairs, slamming the front door behind her.

I watched from the window.

I watched her get on the bike and slowly pedal it out on to the road.

I watched her as she whizzed off down the hill, her hair billowing out behind her from underneath the helmet.

And I heard her whoop for joy, a cry of freedom.
A girl, alive.

Two days later, Grandma Woebegone died, passing over to the other side to join Grandpa Woebegone.

But it turned out that the helmet was not the only thing she had left Greta. Much to her parents' fury, Grandma left *everything* to Greta: the house, the money, all the mementoes of her life.

The first thing Greta spent her newfound wealth on was a splendid new gravestone for Percy, which she went to every week and laid flowers on.

The next thing she bought was a yoga studio for her mother. Greta was a far better person than I ever was.

Let us just say there were strange tales told of the yoga lessons that Greta's mother taught in her new studio. How they were often interrupted by icy draughts, bells ringing by themselves and students running out screaming, claiming that they had heard terrifying whispers that crawled inside their mind like maggots . . .

Greta still missed her grandparents desperately, of course, but she was happy that they were together. And she was happy in the knowledge that she would see them again one day.

And until that day she had me for company.

Wolfgang van Bach-Storey. Musician. Worm farmer. Ghost. And friend.

Family Woebegone

Acknowledgements

Firstly, I must thank my editor, Ben Horslen – although frankly getting to edit my novels is all the thanks he needs. He really is the most fortunate man in publishing, although I'm not too sure he quite recognizes the level of honour bestowed upon him. Huge thanks to Pippa Shaw, Jennie Roman, Steph Barrett and Leena Lane, who correct all the mistakes Ben makes.

One is also obligated to thank one's agent – they tend to get extremely grumpy otherwise. So – thank you to my agent, Julia Churchill. It is widely recognized that literary agents are the most important, intelligent, kind, wise and humble people in publishing, and Julia helps prove this. Julia also cooks and likes donkeys, which is a double bonus. And huge thanks to Gosia Jezierska at A M Heath who always makes me smile!

I'd like to thank my illustrator, Sarah Horne. She saves the world from seeing my illustrations, for which all should be grateful. She brings everything alive with her pen, and I am in awe of her talent.

I'd like to thank everybody at Puffin. In no particular order of importance: Ben Hughes – eurgh. Way too talented and too good-looking, which is just annoying; Clare Blanchfield and Phoebe Williams – the real powerhouses in the team, so I have to be nice to them. Thanks, both – I genuinely appreciate all your hard work; Kat Baker, Toni Budden and all the soldiers in the sales teams; Alice Grigg and all in the rights team; Ken De Silva; Adam Webling; and Francesca Dow, who dresses spectacularly AND allows me to keep writing books. Thank you all. It's an honour to be part of the team.

Thanks to everybody in the children's book community – you really are too numerous to mention and I have been told these acknowledgements have to be in tomorrow morning and it's really late so I can't possibly name you all. But thank you.

And finally, thanks to Claire, Peter and all at my second home at RCW, and especially Honor for keeping me sane.

Loved Greta?

Meet Uma –
the girl with a
million questions . . .

. . . and Athena –
the AI with all
the answers . . .

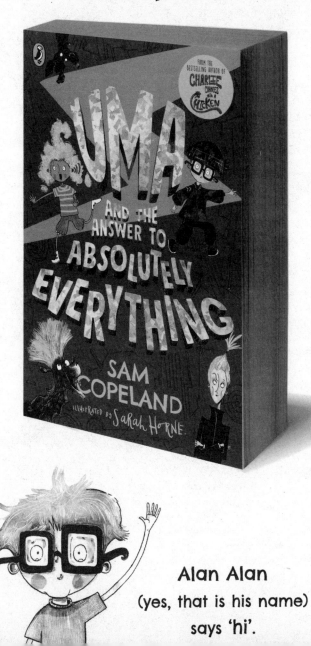

Alan Alan
(yes, that is his name)
says 'hi'.